YORK NOTES

General Editors: Professor A.N. Jeffares (*Univer...*
of Stirling) & Professor Suheil B~~...~~
University of Beirut)

Charles Dickens

OLIVER TWIST

Notes by Suzanne Brown
BA (MOUNT HOLYOKE) PH D (DUBLIN)

LONGMAN
YORK PRESS

14846
823

YORK PRESS
Immeuble Esseily, Place Riad Solh, Beirut.

LONGMAN GROUP UK LIMITED
Longman House, Burnt Mill, Harlow,
Essex CM20 2JE, England
and Associated Companies throughout the world.

First published 1981
Third impression 1989

ISBN 0-582-78254-6

Produced by Longman Group (FE) Ltd
Printed in Hong Kong

Contents

Part 1

Introduction

The life and work of Charles Dickens

Charles Dickens was born to improvident but interesting parents, on 7 February 1812, in Portsmouth, a busy seaport on the south coast of England. His life was to be a great popular success story, publicised by himself, but from the first he was surrounded by failures. He was named after his mother's father, who had fled the country two years before Dickens was born, because his embezzling from the Naval Pay Office had been uncovered and he was threatened with legal proceedings. The troubles of Charles's parents were all too obvious to him as they slid down the social scale in the years of his childhood.

As an adult, Dickens felt persistently hemmed in by the failures of others: firstly, the parents whose frequent financial troubles were a constant strain on both his purse and his patience, and secondly, his wife, whose inadequate housekeeping and limited abilities deeply frustrated him, and lastly, his disappointing children, whose inability to make their ways in the world mystified their self-made father. But the energy he did not encounter in his closest relationships he infused into the characters who people his books. It is one of Dickens's most outstanding literary skills; his characters linger in the mind long after his rather preposterous plots are forgotten.

Dickens met many sorts of people on the bumpy road of his childhood. His father John was a naval pay clerk at Portsea when Charles was born. They lived there until Charles was two, first in a small lower-middle-class terraced house, and later in something cheaper. In 1814 John Dickens was appointed to a London post and in 1816 to one of the principal naval dockyards, in Chatham at the mouth of the river Medway in Kent, thirty miles south-east of London. There they lived first in a pleasant, middle-class house (2 Ordnance Terrace) and then later at a less attractive address (St Mary's Place). In Ordnance Terrace young Charles had a nursemaid, Mary Weller, whose marvellous and often terrifying tales he remembered all his life. Children's fairy tales filled his imagination with vivid and grotesque creatures, like the wolf disguised as Red Riding Hood's grandmother or the Yellow Dwarf from *Mother Bunch*. Best of all he loved *The Arabian Nights*, to which he would make reference all his life. The New Testament was also brought frequently to his attention and though young Dickens loathed church preaching, he found the parables of Jesus appealing and memorable. His own reading branched out to include eighteenth-century novels such as *Roderick Random* (1748) by Tobias Smollett (1721–71), *Don Quixote* (1605) by Miguel de Cervantes (1547–1616) and *Tom Jones* (1749) by Henry Fielding (1707–54). His mother and her sister were instructing him and the other children at home, a process which Charles enjoyed. In one of his rare tributes to his mother he said that she awakened his first desire for knowledge and his earliest passion for reading. These Chatham days included the fun of impromptu magic lantern shows and happy musical 'productions' with his elder sister Fanny, who later went to the Royal Academy of Music. He also loved spoofing with his amiable younger brother Fred, who lived with him later, during the first years of Charles's marriage. He loved outings to the Theatre Royal, where he saw the great clown Grimaldi, as well as some poor productions of Shakespeare. Pleasant afternoons were also spent walking with his father, whose rambling, cheerful conversation made the world seem a happy place.

The family's move to London in 1822 ended that period of innocent, sheltered happiness which Dickens would always believe was the right of every child. Pressed financially, the Dickens family crowded father, mother, six children, a lodger, and a young orphan maid-of-all-work into a house of four rooms. Yet Dickens's parents kept up their hopeful spirits and their pretence of gentility with a persistence that Dickens half scorned and half admired. He created many characters who live in this half-light of back streets with infinite social gradations, characters whose aspirations and assumptions are often comic. He had time to observe many of his neighbours, for he was no longer sent to school. But the humiliating idleness which angered and frustrated him was followed by worse trouble. The family moved to a more expensive house because Mrs Dickens hoped to run a boarding-school. The only evidence of it was a brass plate on their front door, and circulars that brought no applications. Their former lodger found young Charles a job labelling bottles in a new boot-blacking factory, and his parents greeted it with enthusiasm. Shortly after that John Dickens was arrested for debts, and put in Marshalsea debtors' prison, where, as was common practice, Mrs Dickens, their young children and the young servant joined him. Fanny was safely in the Royal Academy of Music, but Charles was sent back to north London to board with other unwanted children in a Mrs Roylance's house. He hated her, he hated his job, he came almost to hate his mother for being so casual about arrangements. The only relief he found was in visiting his family on Sundays, where he shared the meals they were able to buy with John Dickens's Custom House salary that slow official channels had not yet withdrawn.

Dickens walked daily across London, going from the factory to the boarding-house. He must have seen many people whose lives seemed as warped and confused as he felt his own to be. When relief came, in the form of a legacy that gave his father enough to pay his debts, Charles had already moved closer to the prison, but still a long walk from the factory. He knew London's streets better than most adults would, yet he was only twelve.

The dazed suffering and bitterness of these months remained inside Dickens's imagination all his adult life. Although Oliver in *Oliver Twist* is seldom allowed to express such complex feelings, he portrays, in his innocent, untainted acceptance of his brutal circumstances, the dark contrast that Dickens felt between what he himself deserved and what he was fated to endure. Perhaps because life now took a turn for the better, and was never so grim again, Dickens's imagination hardened into the crystal through which a pained child sees the world of corrupt, bustling, grotesque adults and fairy-godmother-like people who occasionally test and rescue young innocents. Dickens despised weakness, particularly in women, for the rest of his life. Yet he also pitied the outcast more than most Victorian gentlemen did. If he became domineering – and he did, in his magazine editorships and at home – he also was stirred to a persistent awareness of social evils and the people who live them out in dreary, frightened days and nights.

His own fortunes rapidly improved. His father enrolled him in Wellington House Academy, which, while not a good school, was at least a way for him to rejoin the Victorian middle class. At fifteen Dickens became a legal clerk, but he learned shorthand in his spare time and soon took his chance as a freelance reporter of Doctors' Commons cases and later of Parliamentary proceedings. Both institutions gave him a contempt for bureaucracy that penetrates all his books, from Oliver's harsh treatment by a Board of Guardians administering the Poor Laws to the fuddled progress of 'Jarndyce *v.* Jarndyce' in *Bleak House* (1853). He reported, first for his uncle's *Mirror of Parliament*, and later also for an evening paper, the *True Sun*. Then he was offered a post on the more powerful *Morning Chronicle*. He began to publish literary sketches as well, first anonymously, and then under the name of Boz. His first book, *Sketches by Boz*, came out in February 1836, when he was twenty-four. But real success came with *Pickwick Papers*, later that year, and then he left reporting for ever. His pride in all he had accomplished sparked the flint of further ambition.

During these same years Dickens was going through a painful adolescent awareness of women. He tried to woo Maria Beadnell, whose family were in banking. They sent her abroad to take her mind off him, and while her ardour cooled his did not. When she rejected his suit, about the time he turned twenty-one, he felt insulted to nearly the same degree as he had when 'put to work with common boys' in the blacking factory. Again the state of mind he endured crystallised, and could be recollected at any time later in his life, with renewed pain. This strange trait gave Dickens an unforgiving personality, but it also enhanced the vivid emotional colouring of his writing.

Dickens married Catherine Hogarth in April 1836. He was proud of her family's social and cultural standing; her father had practised law before turning to journalism, and had been a friend of the famous historical novelist Sir Walter Scott (1771–1832). A year later Dickens could match his own standing as a very popular writer against this and find his in-laws wanting. Perhaps in this came the first upheaval in a marriage that was to stagger along, with an increasing family, until 1858 when Dickens and his wife separated. Catherine's younger sister Mary and Dickens's younger brother Fred both lived with the young couple, a common practice in those days. But Dickens found himself emotionally involved with Mary beyond all his expectation, and when she died suddenly in 1837, he felt he had received another wound he would carry all his life. Dickens's young female heroines are notoriously unreal and uninteresting. Many critics have wondered if Dickens's hyper-sensitivity to his mother's faults, to Maria Beadnell's rejection, and to Mary Hogarth's death killed for ever his adult interest in women's personalities.

By now Dickens's character and traits were basically formed. The tensions within the self-made man who remembered being the lost child and the unsatisfied husband, who remembered being the ardent lover, both hurt and stimulated him the rest of his life. His own stormy human relationships indicate the tremendous emotional energy of the man who invested the novel with a greater number of memorable characters than any other writer before or since. In his plots, as in his own life, he infused melodrama with high intelligence, and in doing so he created a new form far more imaginatively rich than the work of his eighteenth-century predecessors Tobias Smollett, Laurence Sterne (1713–68), and Henry Fielding.

Dickens's first big success came with *Pickwick Papers*, which was published in monthly instalments from April 1836. Before *Pickwick Papers* was finished, he was writing *Oliver Twist*, which began appearing monthly in February 1837. Although he resigned from the *Morning Chronicle*, his workload was heavy; he was editing *Bentley's Miscellany*, the new magazine in which *Oliver Twist* was being printed. Yet before *Oliver Twist* was completed, *Nicholas Nickleby* was appearing, published by Chapman and Hall. By 1841, he began bringing *Barnaby Rudge* into print. This proliferation of highly entertaining novels, and their publication in modestly priced sections, gave Dickens a popular appeal that he has never lost.

During this time he had many financial burdens. His family was growing; he had by now three children, and his parents were financially distressed. He tried to respond to these obligations by editing a weekly publication, *Master Humphrey's Clock*, with contributors other than himself to supplement his own serialised story. The first issues did not sell well, and Dickens felt he must boost sales by expanding the sketches he was contributing to it into a full-length novel, *The Old Curiosity Shop* (1840). This fairytale story of a child's sufferings and death was extremely popular. It was followed by *Barnaby Rudge* (1841), also first appearing in *Master Humphrey's Clock*, a tale set in the recent past of the 1780 Gordon Riots.

Dickens then began the habit of travelling that was to refresh and stimulate him for the rest of his life. Free from writing commitments, he spent six months in America in 1842. He used his impressions in later chapters of *Martin Chuzzlewit*, the serialised novel he had begun to publish in January of that year. *Master Humphrey's Clock* had finished in 1841 with the end of *Barnaby Rudge*, but a new popular scheme occurred to Dickens: a series of annual Christmas books. The first, *A Christmas Carol* (1843), was a huge success. It was followed by *The Chimes* (1844), *The Cricket on the Hearth* (1845), *The Battle of Life* (1846) and *The Haunted Man* (1848). In 1850 he began the journal *Household Words*. This direct contact with his audience eased Dickens's hunger for affection, and he continued editing first this journal, and then its successor (from 1859) *All the Year Round*, until his death.

In 1844 he travelled to Italy, but returned home to read *The Chimes* aloud to a circle of friends. He went back to Genoa through Paris, and when he took the wrong boat from Marseilles, the steamer he should have taken was delayed until the famous author could be brought back to port and safely brought aboard. He had indeed achieved renown, and was becoming addicted to the sense of a great audience held in his sway.

When the family returned to England, Dickens produced *Pictures From Italy* (1846), something close to a travelogue. His mixed feelings about the past had been intensified by travel, and later in *Household Words* (1851, 1852, 1853) he published *A Child's History of England*.

In 1846 after a few weeks of editing a new newspaper, *The Daily News*, Dickens quarrelled with others involved, and resigned. Restless again, he set off for Switzerland. But *Dombey and Son* progressed only slowly, and he moved in October 1846 to Paris, which became his periodic place of refuge throughout the 1850s. *Dombey and Son* (1848) was a sombre novel about Dombey's search for an heir. Then in February 1849 he began his most autobiographical novel, *David Copperfield*. At the same time, Dickens was helping Miss Angela Burdett Coutts to run a home for fallen women, a project in which he was sincerely involved until his separation from his wife in 1858 caused his friendship with Miss Coutts to falter. Both *Dombey and Son* and *David Copperfield* were successful as serials and as volumes. They followed Dickens's usual procedure of serial publication, and then volume reprint when the serialisation was concluded.

His next novel, *Bleak House*, began appearing in November 1851. It was a social novel, without much of the grotesque comedy Dickens's readers had come to regard as a feature of his characteristic idiom. It derived great strength from the integrity of its structure; neither dangling plots nor extra characters distract the reader. Its story indicted the careless upper class whose languor was leaving England without forceful leadership or needed reforms. His next novel, *Hard Times*, appearing weekly from April 1854, attacked the new industrial profiteers and the strikers who rebelled against them. Dickens's own social perceptions were becoming more despairing, and this novel, with its hard views, reflected his own depression. *Little Dorrit*, appearing monthly from the end of 1855, also castigated English life but perhaps with more humour.

Dickens had taken to public readings and amateur theatricals in the mid-1850s, both as a release for his dynamic energy and as a way to raise money for charities, at a time when private charity seemed to him to be the only way to remedy social evils without bringing worse evils into being. On a theatrical tour in 1857 he met a young actress, Ellen Ternan, who unwittingly charmed him and caused him to feel the sadness of his fading marriage unbearably. In June 1858 his separation from his wife was final – and public, for he printed a letter in *Household Words*, defending his action. From then on he lived mainly in Gad's Hill, Kent, a pleasant country house. His sister-in-law Georgina Hogarth was the mistress of his household and foster-mother to all his children except Charles, who stayed with Catherine Dickens.

London became distasteful to Dickens, but he satisfied his need for social life in a variety of ways. One of these was the giving of public readings of excerpts from his own works. These tours were very successful and their success deeply gratified him. It came at a time when his separation was disturbing old friendships, and causing a rift with his publishers, Bradbury and Evans. He returned to publishing with Chapman and Hall, sold up *Household Words*, and incorporated it into a new magazine, *All the Year Round* (1859). To launch this magazine, Dickens serialised a new novel, *A Tale of Two Cities*, in it, and followed this with a serialisation of his young friend Wilkie Collins's (1824–89) novel *The Woman in White* (1860). *A Tale of Two Cities* was uncharacteristically romantic in tone and lacked the social breadth of *Bleak House* or the dark humour of his earlier writing. *Great Expectations* (1861), his next novel, seemed to include his developing seriousness of tone without sacrificing his liveliness or range. He soon began another novel, *Our Mutual Friend*, but complications in his private life and failing health made its progress slow, and it did not begin to appear until 1865. A troubled novel, set in his own time, it also used the tight style towards which Dickens was moving. His last novel, *The Mystery of Edwin Drood*, Dickens did not live to finish. Worn out by public readings, and by a last ill-advised American tour, Dickens died on 9 June 1870. He was then, and still is, the best-loved and most widely read of all the English novelists.

A note on the text

Oliver Twist ran as a monthly serial in *Bentley's Miscellany* from February 1837 until midsummer 1838, and was subsequently published by Bentley. In June 1840 Dickens paid Bentley fifteen hundred pounds for his copyright and seven hundred and fifty pounds for the remaining copies and the Cruikshank plates. This money was provided by Chapman and Hall, his subsequent publishers. They deducted it from three thousand pounds that they were paying Dickens for a six-month copyright to *Barnaby Rudge*. There have been many editions since then, most including the original Cruikshank illustrations. A full edition of Dickens currently in print is the *Oxford Illustrated Dickens*. The fullest edition is the *Centenary Edition of the Works of Charles Dickens*, Chapman and Hall, London; Charles Scribner's Sons, New York, 1911.

Part 2

Summaries
of OLIVER TWIST

A general summary

Oliver Twist tells the adventures of a young waif, born in a workhouse of an unknown, unmarried mother who died delivering him into the world. It briefly describes his early hardships and tells how the workhouse Board of Guardians then apprentices him to an undertaker, from whose grisly service he runs away. He gets as far as the outskirts of London where he meets a seemingly helpful youngster, who introduces him into a gang of young criminals. They are ruled by a wily, heartless man named Fagin, who trains them as thieves. Also associated with Fagin are young adults, some of whom are involved in housebreaking, others in thievery or prostitution. One of the girls, Nancy, takes a liking to young Oliver. Oliver is soon taken on a thieving expedition, but in his naïvety is caught, while the other boys run off with the stolen goods. He is tried in court, but acquitted. He faints and is taken home by the man who lost his property. There he remains, sick, for some time. While he is in this house his rescuer, Mr Brownlow, notices his remarkable resemblance to a portrait of a young woman on the wall in Oliver's room.

Oliver's ill-luck is not over. When he is sent on a message alone, he is kidnapped by Nancy and her housebreaker lover Bill Sikes, and brought back to Fagin's gang. After a period of total isolation, Oliver is sent out again, this time with Sikes. They go to a house outside London, but again Oliver is seen during the crime. This time he is shot. Sikes drags him off, but leaves him in a ditch. Next morning, Oliver drags himself to the house, the home of Mrs Maylie and her adopted niece Rose. Again, Oliver is taken in, believed, and protected. Again he recovers. But this time he meets a more menacing figure, Monks, whom he later sees with Fagin.

Meanwhile Mr Bumble, a parish official who knew Oliver from early childhood, has chanced to see an advertisement from Brownlow requesting any information regarding Oliver, and rushes to tell Brownlow his low opinion of the boy. Bumble also chances to meet Monks, who pumps him for information regarding Oliver's birth and real identity. Bumble himself has little to give, but his wife, the workhouse matron, had attended the deathbed of a pauper who nursed Oliver's mother, and who revealed to Mrs Bumble some suggestive clues. A pawn ticket Oliver's mother was holding when she died yielded a locket and gold ring. These Mrs Bumble sells to Monks, who throws them into a river.

Rose Maylie, like Nancy before her, is very attracted to Oliver and he returns her affection. Her life is saddened by an unfulfilled love for Mrs Maylie's son, Harry, whom she cannot marry because of the blight of uncertainty about her own birth. Mr Brownlow reappears in London after an absence of some months, and is spotted in a street by Oliver, just after Rose has had a totally unexpected encounter with Nancy. Nancy has learned of Oliver's real danger from Monks and Fagin, and has also heard Rose's name and temporary hotel address mentioned by the two, so she bravely seeks Rose out to tell her all she knows. Rose, deeply perplexed, turns to Mr Brownlow for help. He is delighted to hear of Oliver's good character, and goes with Rose to meet Nancy again. The first time Nancy fails to keep the appointment; the second time she is followed by a spy for Fagin, who reports back that she is informing on him. Nancy is murdered by Sikes for her part in Oliver's rescue. Sikes, unreasoning and full of rage, believes that he is betrayed. After her death he goes on the run, until his own violent death.

Meanwhile, Brownlow and others apprehend Monks, and privately force a confession from him, in return for keeping away from the police. Fagin is captured, as an accomplice of Sikes, tried, and hanged. Oliver learns from Monks his real identity. He is Rose's nephew, the son of her unfortunate older sister, who was betrayed in love by a weak friend of Brownlow. He is Monks's step-brother, for Brownlow's friend was actually married to Monks's mother.

Thus Oliver and Rose acquire identity. Rose and Harry settle their affairs happily, the Bumbles are disgraced, and the criminal gang is in ruins. Oliver begins a new life, adopted by Mr Brownlow as his son.

Oliver Twist has been a popular novel since Dickens first published it serially in *Bentley's Miscellany* in 1837–8. However, the initial reactions of the intellectual critics of his day were more mixed. Thackeray took it to be one of the 'Newgate novels' that sensationalised crimes of violence, and the *Quarterly* questioned 'a series of representations which must familiarise the rising generation with the haunts, deeds, language, and characters of the very dregs of the community'. Dickens himself dismissed these reactions as snobbery. He believed that, to tell the truth, he must first have an audience; and he enjoyed his power of entertaining them. The more serious purpose of the novel was effected if he stirred his readers' imaginations and emotions to recognise, perhaps with a twinge of fear, how thin the line was between respectability and the horrible life of the outcast. In portraying Sikes, Fagin, and particularly Nancy, Dickens showed how corrupting the criminal's life was, how the very fabric of personality became eaten away. Normal, responsible relationships were replaced by the servile love Nancy has for Sikes, by the desperate wavering of her loyalty to Oliver, or by the false give-and-take of Sikes and Fagin. But he allowed pity to penetrate even into Fagin's death cell, so that the reader seeing Fagin go bewildered and dazed to his hanging could sense the horror and the blank meaninglessness of such a death. Throughout the novel, Oliver's impressionable mind is like a mirror reflecting the innocence and corruption that he meets. He makes little of what he sees, but stumbles blindly toward his own good fortune. He could die a criminal death each time he is captured. His helplessness is echoed in Nancy's tale of her own past, poured out to Rose Maylie, whose life is also nearly blighted by events beyond her control. These figures move in and out of a landscape of teeming activity, yet the novel suggests how few people can do much to improve their situations. Their activity cannot remedy the evils from which they suffer, or rescue them to lead happy, useful lives. Dickens's poor childhood and frightened months as a blacking boy colour the fear expressed in *Oliver Twist* with an intense shading of gloom. It is a moving and unhappy book, despite Oliver's changed fortune. Oliver is given future happiness, but many, including many dead, were not rescued by the weak efforts they made. Moreover, Oliver the boy thief has been robbed for ever of the childhood peace of mind which should have been his, by the casual brutality of his society and the responding scheming brutality of the anti-social society of thieves. The book offers, instead of a hero like the jaunty youths of eighteenth-century episodic novels, a battered waif who, for the rest of his life, will honour unredeemed dead, and remember fear.

Detailed summaries

Chapter 1: Treats of the Place where Oliver Twist was Born, and of the Circumstances attending his Birth

Oliver is born to an unwed girl, in a workhouse. Her origins, and his, are shrouded in obscurity.

COMMENTARY: The rather arch tone of this opening chapter thinly disguises the feelings of pity and sadness Dickens hopes to arouse in his readers, as he describes the early days of Oliver's life in the workhouse. Almost every parish in England had a workhouse, a place where those too poor to shelter themselves could live and be provided with a meagre diet in return for doing hard physical work. However, in 1834, three years before *Oliver Twist* was written, a new, harsh reform of their administration was effected. From then, all those seeking relief food had to live in the workhouse; 'outdoor' relief was abolished. Conditions were intended to be worse than a very badly paid worker would endure, so that only the desperate would ask for admittance. The newly centralised administration had a Board of three Commissioners, who in turn appointed Regional Assistants. Parishes, the natural units based on villages, were grouped together in Unions, each with a large central workhouse. Boards of Guardians were elected by the property-owners, whose taxes were to pay for the relief. Men, women, and children were housed separately, special dress was worn, visitors were infrequent, and, until 1842, all meals were eaten in silence. The able-bodied did hard physical work, but in these harsh conditions not many stayed able-bodied long. Oliver is born in an old poorhouse, but the workhouse he goes to as a boy is of the new sort.

England had a huge class of labouring poor folk, and, below them, what the Victorian social investigator Henry Mayhew (1812–87)* termed 'those who cannot work' and 'those who will not work'. Oliver begins his life in these low orders, and spends most of his childhood as one of 'those who cannot work' being tempted by 'those who will not work'. Dickens introduces here the tragic injustice of such poor folk's situation, as dramatically as he can:

> What an excellent example of the power of dress, young Oliver Twist was! Wrapped in the blanket which had hitherto formed his only covering, he might have been the child of a nobleman or a beggar; it would have been hard for the haughtiest stranger to have assigned him his proper station in society. But now that he was enveloped in the old calico robes which had grown yellow in the same service, he was badged and ticketed, and fell into his place at once – a parish child – the orphan of a workhouse – the humble, half-starved drudge – to be cuffed and buffeted through the world – despised by all, and pitied by none.

The tone and vocabulary, those of a middle-class dinner-table anecdote, are intended to shock. They also suggest that the writer is no dangerous working-class agitator, but one of the protected middle class himself. Dickens often uses this manner when describing the terrible sufferings of the poor. Beneath its surface his intense emotions are a powerful undercurrent.

NOTES AND GLOSSARY:

churchwarden: lay parish official whose main duties concern the temporal and financial affairs of the church

---

*Though he wrote novels in collaboration with his brother Augustus he is now mainly remembered for his social survey *London Labour and the London Poor* (1837–62). See p. 21.

Chapter 2: Treats of Oliver Twist's Growth, Education, and Board

Oliver, having spent his early childhood farmed out to a woman keen for a weekly income, is now brought to the workhouse. He soon disgraces himself, and is offered as an apprentice to anyone willing to have him.

COMMENTARY: Here the reader sees the flashes of grotesque, black humour that mark and brighten every novel Dickens wrote. Young Oliver is farmed out to a poor woman whose slim resources only spur her enterprise. She half-starves babies in care of the parish, and pockets part of the money provided to feed them. Instead of direct anger Dickens mockingly paraphrases her own self-defence. She was convinced that 'sevenpence-halfpenny's worth per week is a good round diet for a child; a great deal may be got for sevenpence-halfpenny, quite enough to overload its stomach, and make it uncomfortable'. Dickens was a great believer in the general greed and self-interest of mankind; his poverty-stricken characters have no special claims to virtue. In that sense he can be seen to be as far from a Marxist* view of society as he is from a Benthamite† one. Although he heartily dislikes the prevalent view of allowing no interference with the struggles of the market place, and valuing all things and people only inasmuch as they are definably useful, Dickens believes that the poor corrupt themselves as often as the rich do; the rich merely sin in greater comfort.

This chapter brings Oliver to the age of nine, the time when his own adventures will begin. Each parish had a beadle, an official who helped to keep discipline. One of his duties was to look in on the children farmed out by the parish, and report back to the Board of Guardians. Mr Bumble is a beadle, full of self-importance and little else. He and Mrs Mann share a conspiratorial gin while they discuss Oliver's history. Mr Bumble explains his alphabetical system of naming parish infants, in which he takes a certain pride. Since the ten pounds reward offered by the parish has not led to any discovery of his real identity, 'Oliver Twist' he must remain, and, childhood over, he must now go to the workhouse. Oliver leaves the other children with a burst of grief. Now the devastating loneliness, which nearly prevents him from developing any personality at all, is truly begun. His invented name, his parish clothes, his friendlessness, all indicate the fragility of his identity.

Oliver then is presented to the local Board of Guardians, who insist on treating him as if he were a rather recalcitrant adult on trial for misdemeanours. This atmosphere of public hostility surrounds the poor

*Karl Marx (1818–93) and Friedrich Engels (1820–95) propounded the theory that actions and human institutions are economically determined, that class struggle is the agency of historical change, and that capitalism will be superseded by communism.
†Jeremy Bentham (1748–1831) the English philosopher and jurist who was a founder of utilitarianism.

folk in the workhouse. Dickens slyly attacks the new system – it provides almost the only divorces available in England, it gives great expense to the parish in burying its victims. But the reduced number of those seeking relief delights the Board.

Dickens creates the unforgettable scene in which Oliver dares to ask for 'more', inspiring his illustrator George Cruikshank (1792–1878) to the execution of an equally memorable caricature drawing. The workhouse master is in charge of moral discipline, yet nothing in his experience has so shocked him as the boy's impudence in asking for more food. It seems to him the very death of gratitude and of right social deference. Others are equally shocked. The Board member 'in the white waistcoat' confidently predicts Oliver will someday be hanged. The result is swift: 'five pounds and Oliver Twist' are offered to anyone willing to have him as an apprentice.

NOTES AND GLOSSARY:

domiciled: resident

experimental philosopher: scientist. Dickens here challenges the 'scientific' economy underlying the new Poor Laws

---

Chapter 3: Relates how Oliver Twist was very near getting a Place, which would not have been a Sinecure

---

This chapter tells how Oliver was first put in solitary confinement for a week and then nearly apprenticed to a chimney sweep. He saves himself by another bold act, appealing directly to the magistrate not to send him away with Mr Gamfield the sweep.

COMMENTARY: In this chapter the reader sees Oliver's first venture into the wider world. He meets two sorts of people he will meet again, the kindly, well-meaning, half-blind magistrate whose personal charity makes him take an interest in the boy, and the greedy, grasping but impoverished sweep who wants to apprentice him. Later in the story, Oliver will meet other kindly middle-class people, and instinctively will appeal to them for help. Other greedy, poor but wicked people will try to apprentice him and he will resist, with diminishing success. His crisis will become more acute, his future will teeter more wildly in the balance. Between the two sorts of people are the callous, lower-middle-class figures like the beadle, Mr Bumble, who always try to buy and sell, whatever the commodity, even if it is boys' futures.

Dickens displays many of his basic attitudes in this chapter. He believes that theft tempts the tormented poor as a way of making something of a living. He sees that the lower-middle class is close enough to the poor to know this about them, and to see their real sufferings, but turns a blind eye, being much more concerned to show how much better they are. The tiny upper-middle class provide most of Dickens's few virtuous characters, but they indulge in a kind of innocence which is socially disastrous. They rise to heights of personal charity and sacrifice, but make no real impact on the vast problems of nineteenth-century England.

NOTES AND GLOSSARY:

incarceration: imprisonment

indentures: written agreements binding an apprentice to his master's service

---

Chapter 4: Oliver, being offered another Place, makes his first Entry into Public Life

---

Oliver is apprenticed to Sowerberry, the parish undertaker, and goes to his new life among the coffins.

COMMENTARY: This chapter opens with a reference to Oliver's possible naval future, and plays darkly again with the notion that the Board wishes Oliver dead. There is a dark shadow over all of *Oliver Twist*, a shadow of the accepted deaths of thousands of poor children and the short, brutal lives of the survivors. Average life expectancy went down in the early phases of the Industrial Revolution; in some slum areas nearly two-thirds of the children died before the age of nine.

Death was the accepted visitor to every tenement. If the Victorians made more of a spectacle of death than is common now, they accepted it more readily as a social fact that the poor die younger. All children were more at risk from childhood diseases than is usual today, but poor children especially so, in overcrowded town dwellings, in insanitary conditions, and unsafe streets, perhaps even in dangerous jobs. They had a chance, but not a probability, of living to become adults. This gruesome truth colours all Dickens's thinking about the poor. He shows how callous it makes some, and how ravaged it leaves others. Dickens, often accused by critics of sentimentality, never actually allows his poor characters a distinguishing heroic virtue, but in Oliver he takes one of their number and endows him with a blind, persistent urge to live that protects him from the forces swirling round him. Blind endurance is a poor child's greatest asset.

Oliver's apprenticeship is to the parochial undertakers. It is all arranged in a conversation between Mr Bumble the beadle and Mr Sowerberry the undertaker, without consulting Oliver's wishes any more than the Board had the first time. Dickens's irony is heavy-handed. Mr Bumble's fine brass button of the Good Samaritan helping the injured man made its first public appearance at an inquest of a tradesman who had starved to death in the cold. He and Mr Sowerberry are at ease with the death of others and joke merrily about small coffins.

Oliver goes unprotestingly to his new employer, but cries out as they near the undertaker's house:

'I am a very little boy, sir; and it is so – so – '
'So what?' inquired Mr Bumble in amazement.
'So lonely, sir! So very lonely!' cried the child. 'Everybody hates me. Oh! sir, don't, don't pray be cross to me!'

After Oliver arrives, Mrs Sowerberry makes it plain that he is not welcomed by her, and he takes his place as the least of all the servants in their establishment. He is fed from the dog's supper, and led down among the coffins to take what rest he can.

NOTES AND GLOSSARY:

| vixenish: | ill-tempered |
| slatternly: | untidy, slovenly |

Chapter 5: Oliver mingles with new Associates. Going to a Funeral for the first Time, he forms an unfavourable Notion of his Master's Business

---

Oliver begins his new duties, and makes new acquaintances. He attends a pauper's funeral.

COMMENTARY: Oliver meets Mr Noah Claypole, a charity-boy who works for the Sowerberrys. He swaggers into Oliver's life, proud of the narrow degree of respectability that separates him from a workhouse child who does not know who his parents were. Noah has his own position to defend. Charlotte, the maid, admires him, and he is perhaps happier than his master, who lives in a mild servitude to his shrewish wife.

Oliver's unhappiness is increased when Mr Sowerberry begins to train him as a mute for children's funerals, a child to march alongside the coffin, part of the pageantry of grief that can be bought. To help him to learn his master's trade, Oliver accompanies Sowerberry as he measures a pauper's corpse, and attends the poor woman's funeral. She gets a shallow grave and four minutes' worth of service. (Dickens based this detail on a funeral he had seen.) Oliver finds the experience horrifying, but his attendance implies a boost to his own status that will make Noah Claypole jealous. The callous and calculating shrewdness of everyone Oliver meets contrasts with his near-silent innocence. Although he is totally unable to take command of his situation or to improve it, he remains curiously untouched by its corrupting and vile influences, in a cocoon of youth.

NOTES AND GLOSSARY:

| charity-boy: | a boy looked after out of parish funds until he can be put to work |

surplice: an outer vestment of white linen worn by a priest during services

---

Chapter 6: Oliver, being goaded by the Taunts of Noah, rouses into Action, and rather astonishes him

---

Oliver rebels against Noah's taunts, and assaults him. He is locked up in the cellar until Mr Bumble can arrive.

COMMENTARY: This chapter begins with the ghastly, grim and rather angry humour that characterises many of Dickens's asides in *Oliver Twist*: 'it was a nice sickly season just at this time. In commercial phrase, coffins were looking up; and, in the course of a few weeks, Oliver acquired a great deal of experience'. Dickens describes the falsity of much grief, the showy weeping that ends when tea is served. He paraphrases the hypocritical professions of resignation, and sarcastically comments that Oliver finds it all to be 'very pleasant and improving'.

Oliver, however, is not sufficiently 'improved' to bear endlessly the jibes of his rival, Noah Claypole. When Noah insults Oliver's mother, the little boy's finer, deeper feelings flush to the surface. He attacks the big bully, who yells for help. The women rush to Noah's rescue, beat Oliver, and throw him into the coalhouse. They then send for Mr Bumble, the beadle; Noah, delighted at Oliver's disgrace, runs this errand himself.

Dickens allows Oliver a flash of honourable temper that would do any boy credit. He shows that despite his obscure origins, Oliver possesses a greater sensitivity and courage than anybody expected of him. These traits are misunderstood; in a poor boy they are out of place. He will be severely punished.

NOTES AND GLOSSARY:
equanimity: serenity
clasp-knife: small knife, the blade of which folds back into the handle when not in use

---

Chapter 7: Oliver continues refractory

Oliver is punished by the beadle and the Sowerberrys. He spends a solitary night, and then leaves the Sowerberrys for ever. He reaches his old home, and sees his friend Dick.

COMMENTARY: This is the chapter in which we perhaps come closest to young Oliver's own nature. His surroundings dominate our impressions in later chapters, whether his luck is up or down. In this chapter he is acting on his own, following for once the impulses of his own heart.

Taunted even by Mrs Sowerberry, beaten by Bumble and Sowerberry, sent in disgrace to his own dark bed, he weeps his heart out. But his courage returns, and he packs up his few things and leaves the Sowerberrys for ever. He goes back to the only home he remembers, the house where he was 'farmed out' with other children too young for the workhouse. There he finds his friend Dick, who is slowly dying. Oliver loves his friend with a passion that Dickens tells the reader will outlast his turmoil of emotions and his changes of fortune. He loves him with a special intensity because the little boy is his only special friend and is in great danger. Dick is part of Oliver's lost childhood. He will never see him again. Later in the story, he will return, to hear that Dick has died. This contrast with a more fortunate child's natural pleasure in his friendships is one way in which Dickens stirs the conscience of his audience, reminding them that for every Oliver who was rescued, hundreds of children died, children as loving and gentle as Oliver himself.

NOTES AND GLOSSARY:
sanguinary: bloodthirsty

Chapter 8: Oliver walks to London. He encounters on the Road a Strange sort of young Gentleman

---

Oliver walks to London. Just outside the city, he makes a new acquaintance, who brings him to Fagin's den.

COMMENTARY: Oliver now meets the Artful Dodger, a child of endearing courage and spirited deviousness. The Dodger is worldly-wise, in a limited way, and is always on the lookout for possible new recruits to the criminal life. He saves Oliver's life; he is the only saviour that life offers Oliver, the only Good Samaritan to whom Oliver can turn. But his is not disinterested kindness. He is in the outer ring of the criminal world that will suck Oliver down like a dark funnel. In 1862 Henry Mayhew published an account of *Those That Will Not Work*; he estimated it as a vast class. He believed that of the labouring poor, only one-third were partially unemployed and another one-third were wholly unemployed. But, in addition to these destitute, he believed there were those who saw crime as a career. He estimated it in London as 12,000 individuals, in England and Wales as 150,000. Mayhew agreed with the Constabulary Commission of 1839 that people were seldom driven to crime by poverty, but took it up because of 'the temptation of obtaining poverty with a less degree of labour than by regular industry'.

Dickens knew he must defend introducing these people into fiction in an unromanticised way. They were easy for his readers to despise or ignore, in life. Subtly he suggests that the urge to feel better than one's fellows and safer from pitfalls exists even in the criminal classes, in their infinite gradations. Oliver is pitied and a little scorned, by the Dodger and his mates.

The Artful Dodger is one of Dickens's great creations. He speaks a slang unknown to Oliver or to most of Dickens's readers. Just as Oliver's unexpectedly refined speech suggests his natural refinement and sensitivity, so the Dodger's language suggests his active, colourful, matey nature. He buys Oliver a meal, and then brings him to Fagin's den, a shabby tenement room. There the old Jew and the boys he keeps as a gang of pickpockets decide to take Oliver in. This is the London underworld, which frightened and fascinated Victorians, in a new light.

NOTES AND GLOSSARY:

chandler: dealer in groceries and small wares

Chapter 9: Containing further Particulars concerning the pleasant old Gentleman, and his hopeful Pupils

---

This chapter gives the reader intimations of the real nature of Fagin's activities, though Oliver remains naïvely confused. He meets Nancy, and begins to settle in.

COMMENTARY: The real horror of Oliver's new situation comes before the reader now as Dickens reveals more of Fagin's shadowy, evil personality. Fagin gloats over booty his boys have stolen, while he thinks Oliver is asleep. He mutters to himself:

> What a fine thing capital punishment is! Dead men never repent; dead men never bring awkward stories to light. Ah, it's a fine thing for the trade! Five of 'em strung up in a row, and none left to play booty, or turn white-livered!

When Fagin realises Oliver might be awake, he waves a knife over the boy. Oliver, inexperienced as he is, still has the wit to notice that Fagin is afraid as well as angry. He is deeply puzzled about Fagin's seeming poverty, considering that he is the proud owner of a hoard of treasure. Fagin admits he is a miser, saving up a little 'property' for his old age. But Oliver's mystification deepens when the Artful Dodger and Charley Bates come into the room, bringing two pocket-books and four handkerchiefs. Although Oliver does not understand it, the 'game' Fagin plays with these two after breakfast portrays in miniature his foxy relationship with the young boys he takes in. While pretending to care for them, he trains them as pickpockets; if they are caught, he hopes they will be hanged quickly, before they breathe a word about him.

Two prostitutes also come into Fagin's den; Oliver considers them 'very nice girls indeed'. Dickens adds 'as no doubt they were'. This remark begins Dickens's creation of Nancy, in whom finer feelings and degraded emotions mix. Alcohol is then produced for the girls, as it was for Oliver when he first arrived. The need for money for drink helps to keep the girls tied to Fagin. As the chapter closes, the reader watches Oliver's muddled innocence slipping into Fagin's eager hands; Fagin begins to mould the boy, giving him his first chance to feel useful to the gang.

NOTES AND GLOSSARY:
corporeal: bodily

Chapter 10: Oliver becomes better acquainted with the Characters of his new Associates; and purchases Experience at a high Price. Being a short, but very important Chapter, in this History

---

Oliver is allowed to go out with the Dodger and Charley Bates. The two young rascals pick a man's pocket but Oliver is blamed, chased, and captured.

COMMENTARY: This chapter allows Oliver another brush with the respectable world, and like all his previous such experiences, it is unhappy. He goes out with the Dodger and Charley Bates to begin 'work'. The real nature of their trade becomes obvious to him when they pick the pocket of a gentleman at a bookstall. He hesitates, horrified; and thus is left to take the blame when the man realises his loss. The cry, 'Stop, thief!' makes Oliver run madly, while the gentleman and a swelling crowd race after him. He is captured and knocked down. Dickens's real sympathy flashes out:

> There is a passion *for hunting something* deeply implanted in the human breast. One wretched breathless child, panting with exhaustion; terror in his looks; agony in his eyes; large drops of perspiration streaming down his face; strains every nerve to make head upon his pursuers; and as they follow on his track, and gain upon him every instant, they hail his decreasing strength with still louder shouts, and whoop and scream with joy. 'Stop, thief!' Ay, stop him for God's sake, were it only in mercy!

The gentleman is pained to see Oliver's terror. He has, himself, run with the bookseller's book still in his hand. But as a good customer he has nothing to fear. Oliver, who has taken nothing, is led off to jail, a new horror at which his young mind reels. Curiously, the gentleman tags along, stirred by sudden compassion for the little boy.

Dickens knows that if Oliver is to keep the reader's sympathy he must remain entirely innocent. He must be an entirely good boy in criminal surroundings, if he is to awaken feelings of anguish about his fate.

However, by developing Oliver's bewilderment and his natural deference to adults, Dickens could allow Oliver the semblance of crime. He could be outcast and innocent at the same time, without becoming so vacuous as to weaken the book.

At every point in the book from now on, the reader feels the pressure of circumstance moulding Oliver's young character. The people he encounters are his main education. Initially, he trusts them all. His trusting eagerness is perhaps Oliver's most unbelievable trait. Given his experiences, it suggests either perpetual hopefulness or stupidity, but Dickens does not want readers to think Oliver stupid. He wants to underline how vulnerable children are to all the adults they live with. When trust fails Oliver, he becomes dazed. Dickens, influenced by his own bitter experience, wants to remind readers that without real help children grow confused, or make for themselves an interpretation of life that can lead to death by accident or by the hangman.

NOTES AND GLOSSARY:

expatiate: sermonise
depredator: thief

Chapter 11: Treats of Mr Fang the Police Magistrate; and furnishes a slight Specimen of his Mode of administering Justice

---

This chapter relates Oliver's trial, sentence and re-trial. As it closes Oliver is unconscious, oblivious of the rescue Fate is affording him. He is taken away in a coach, in the care of Mr Brownlow, the gentleman Fagin's boys had robbed.

COMMENTARY: Oliver's first experience of State justice is no better than his early experience of State charity had been. He is hustled into court despite the gentleman's wish to abandon the charge. The magistrate is notorious for bad decisions, and 'if he were not really in the habit of drinking rather more than was exactly good for him, he might have brought an action against his countenance for libel, and have recovered damages'. He is out of temper and insults Mr Brownlow, the old gentleman, as freely as he dares. Oliver faints in the dock, succumbing to strain and sickness, but is summarily found guilty and sentenced none the less. The case re-opens when the bookseller appears and relates the truth. Oliver is thus rescued, and, still unconscious, is put on the pavement outside. Mr Brownlow and the bookseller then take him away in a hired coach. They belong to a safer, happier world than Oliver has yet entered, but the kindly old man decides to take an interest in Oliver. By this private charity, real hope for Oliver can begin.

Dickens's anger at the awful cells for people charged and awaiting trial, and his scorn for the magistrates who can daily cause miscarriages of justice with impunity, break out of the narrative, in direct attack. When the storyteller occasionally breaks off and makes a direct appeal to his readers' consciences, it is dramatic and very effective. Dickens rarely does this, just often enough to keep his readers aware of the reality of the sufferings he describes in fiction. In the near fairytale description of Oliver's rescue by the kindly intervention of the bookseller and the old gentleman, this interruption reminds readers of the many children no one rescues, who go bewildered into the terrible circumstances of prison. Mayhew reported that children began to learn thieving from stalls at the age of six or seven, helped in a rough way by adult thieves. They vied with one another in skill, and the best became sneaksmen (robbers of shop-tills), or even swell mobsmen (pickpockets). Occasionally they assisted housebreakers. These children seldom saw themselves as doing wrong, and viewed prison as a risk of their trade, but few of them were really prepared for its sufferings. Dickens, who was writing before Mayhew, seems to be as close to the truth as that social investigator was.

NOTES AND GLOSSARY:

fogle-hunter: pickpocket

Chapter 12: In which Oliver is taken better Care of, than he ever was before. And in which the Narrative reverts to the merry old Gentleman and his youthful Friends

---

Oliver recovers, under the kind care of Mr Brownlow and his housekeeper Mrs Bedwin. He startles them by his resemblance to a portrait they have of a young and beautiful woman. Meanwhile the Dodger and Charley Bates have returned without Oliver to Fagin.

COMMENTARY: This is the crucial chapter in Oliver's progress into the Victorian middle class. He recovers slowly from a wasting fever, under the care of Mr Brownlow's old housekeeper Mrs Bedwin. When he first wakes he tells her of his mother, whose kind, happy face has haunted his dreams. This domestic piety affirms that Oliver's natural place is in the secure family of happy and settled position.

At this point in the novel Dickens writes easily and spaciously, with time for pleasant little caricatures of the doctor and the night nurse who care for Oliver. He also takes time to describe the child lying awake, seeing the shadows the rushlight throws on the wall and the wallpaper pattern it illuminates. The pace is slow and easy, as it is when sickness gives way to gradual recovery.

But the style then becomes brisker, as Mrs Bedwin bustles about getting Oliver ready for Mr Brownlow's visit. When the good old gentleman does come in, he is much struck by Oliver's resemblance to a woman's portrait that hangs on his wall. We have the first intimation of the coincidences that will reveal Oliver's true identity.

Meanwhile the Dodger and Charley Bates, having cut away from the chase after Oliver, have made for Fagin's den – but not without fear of his reaction to their losing his new pupil. They don't give Oliver a thought. Not even casual pity disturbs them; the reader is shown how thin and easily snapped are the ties that group the thieves together into their casual band.

NOTES AND GLOSSARY:

lineaments:	features
circumlocutions:	long-winded, roundabout expressions
contingency:	possible event
saveloy:	a kind of sausage

Chapter 13: Some new Acquaintances are introduced to the intelligent Reader; connected with whom various pleasant Matters are related, appertaining to this History

---

The thieves review their situation, and fear Oliver will tell someone about them. Nancy goes to the prison to find him, but is told he was taken away, ill, by the gentleman who had been robbed. She reports to Fagin, who then orders that Oliver should be immediately found and kidnapped.

COMMENTARY: As if to confirm the impression that self-interest is the only real bond among the thieves, the boys fight with Fagin about losing Oliver to the police. Bill Sikes the housebreaker enters just in time to get the contents of a beerpot hurled over him. Sikes kicks his dog across the room. He declares that he would have murdered Fagin long ago if he'd been apprenticed to him, and the Jew cowers. Sikes jokes about Fagin's poisoning the proffered beer, but Dickens adds:

> This was said in jest; but if the speaker could have seen the evil leer with which the Jew bit his pale lip as he turned round to the cupboard, he might have thought the caution not wholly unnecessary, or the wish (at all events) to improve upon the distiller's ingenuity not very far from the old gentleman's heart.

The real picture of a thieves' den is complete.

They all decide to uncover what Oliver has told the police, but none is keen to undertake the task. Two girls come in, and one, Nancy, is coaxed and bullied by Sikes into agreeing to go. This is the first time the reader sees Bill Sikes and Nancy together, but it is immediately clear that she cares for him. She is a plucky girl, and enters into the part of the innocent sister, inquiring after Oliver, with gusto, once she has agreed to it.

She goes past the cells in which prisoners are locked up for vagrancy or for unlicensed hawking, whom Dickens bitterly divides between those imprisoned for not trying to make a living and those imprisoned for trying. The casual cruelty of the courts is very evident. Nancy finds out from the prison officer that Oliver has been taken away by Mr Brownlow. When she returns to Fagin and reports this, he sends them all out to kidnap Oliver, while he remains alone, concealing his secret hoard of watches and jewellery beneath his clothes, to take with him when he goes out that night.

Dickens begins one of his powerful themes: that evil makes each person totally isolated, breaking up all the natural bonds of community. The grotesque, folk-tale figure of Fagin, who keeps goods hidden from those who work for him at the risk of their lives, and the sad prospect of Oliver, who is being hunted down by the gang of criminals, send a shiver of horror through the reader.

NOTES AND GLOSSARY:

antipathy: aversion
encomiums: praises

Chapter 14: Comprising further Particulars of Oliver's Stay at Mr Brownlow's. With the remarkable Prediction which one Mr Grimwig uttered concerning him, when he went out on an Errand

---

Oliver, now recovered, nearly tells his own story to Mr Brownlow. However, Mr Grimwig arrives and challenges Brownlow to test Oliver by sending him on an errand, with money.

COMMENTARY: This chapter shows the uncertainty of Oliver's new standing as a member of the respectable middle class. He is interviewed by Mr Brownlow, who instinctively likes and trusts him. Mr Brownlow speaks of his own sad past efforts to benefit others, about which the reader will hear more, later in the story. Warning Oliver not to betray his trust, he asks for the boy's story.

Just as Oliver is about to begin, they are interrupted by the arrival of Brownlow's friend Grimwig, an eccentric with a rough tongue and a warm heart. Grimwig's love of argument makes him oppose Brownlow's good opinion of Oliver. They agree to send Oliver on an errand, as a kind of test of his integrity. As the chapter closes, they are sitting waiting for his return.

NOTES AND GLOSSARY:

expatiated: talked wanderingly and at length

Chapter 15: Showing how very fond of Oliver Twist, the merry old Jew and Miss Nancy were

---

Sikes meets Fagin to get payment for a robbery. Nancy joins them, and after a time leaves with Sikes. Along their way they meet Oliver, out on his errand. Pretending to onlookers that he is their brother, they drag him off.

COMMENTARY: Sikes, very drunk, is fighting with his dog in a pub, as this chapter opens. They are interrupted by Fagin, who inadvertently lets the dog out, and then comes in for Bill's curses himself. Fagin fears Bill Sikes, but has power over him as well, for the Jew whose pub they are in looks to Fagin when Bill wants another drink, and when he calls for Nancy. Each thief casts what nets of power he can over others in the hope of cheating the hangman. Fagin brings Bill Sikes money, but prevents Nancy from telling Bill what she has learned of Oliver. Nancy seems, despite her abilities, to be afraid of both men and ready to do what she is told. She leaves with Sikes. By an unhappy coincidence they encounter Oliver, running his errand, and seize him, telling everyone he is their young runaway brother. So Oliver is carried off again, into the dark world of back streets, while those who befriended him wait anxiously for him to return. Although he cries out and struggles, the watching crowd assumes the child is wrong and the adults are right, an assumption seldom if ever justified in any novel by Dickens. Knowing the hard natures of the thieves better by now, the reader fears for Oliver. Because he has seen how fragile the trust extended to Oliver by Brownlow is, the reader can have little hope that Oliver will again be rescued.

NOTES AND GLOSSARY:

sovereigns: old gold coins worth a pound sterling

Chapter 16: Relates what became of Oliver Twist after he had been claimed by Nancy

---

Oliver is taken by Bill and Nancy, past the jail where some old acquaintances of theirs will be hanged next day, to a thieves' hideout. There he meets again the boys who tricked him and the old master, Fagin. Sikes is paid for delivering Oliver. Oliver makes one attempt to get away, but is attacked by Sikes's dog. Nancy intervenes. She also protects him from Fagin, almost frightening the men by her passion.

COMMENTARY: Dragged away by Sikes and Nancy, in fear of them and of the fierce dog which is Bill Sikes's constant companion, Oliver lets himself be led back to the thieves' den.

Dickens builds up a dramatic impression of two sections of London, only streets apart, one a ramshackle, impoverished den of thieves, the other a comfortable area of town houses. They co-exist, the first making occasional raids on the second. Oliver is drawn to both, and may end up in either. The dark, foggy night closes over him like water over someone drowning. He does not know where he is. A worse darkness is closing over some of the fellow-thieves; Nancy talks with Bill about the hangings next morning. He becomes almost jealous that they excite her agitated sorrow, and the reader sees that he cares for Nancy, in a passionate, reckless way.

A greater surprise is Nancy's show of feeling for Oliver, when he is first panicking in the thieves' den. He screams and tries to escape. Sikes is all for letting the dog pull him down, but Nancy throws the door shut and will not let Sikes and the dog pass. Oliver is recaptured by Fagin, the Artful Dodger and Master Bates. Fagin starts to beat Oliver with a club, but Nancy grabs it and throws it in the fire. Hatred of their cruelty torments her, mixing with her own recklessness and despair. Sikes swears at her, and insults her, which rouses her further, to an agony of remorse for her share in kidnapping Oliver. Her own history spills out: she was put to thieving for Fagin as a child younger than Oliver, and has been in Fagin's clutches ever since. She struggles when Sikes grabs her, and faints. Oliver is made to change back into the identical rags he thought he had got rid of by seeing them sold to a pedlar. He undresses sadly, as Fagin is speaking about women with characteristic calculation. The reader is left to wonder what Nancy's emotions will cost her.

NOTES AND GLOSSARY:

Bartlemy time: the season of St Bartholomew's Fair, in the late summer

---

Chapter 17: Oliver's Destiny continuing unpropitious, brings a Great Man to London to injure his Reputation

---

Mr Bumble visits Oliver's old home and sees Dick, who expresses a wish to leave a loving message for Oliver after his death. For this Dick is severely reprimanded. Mr Bumble goes to London to appear in a court case, and while there sees Brownlow's advertisement requesting information about Oliver Twist. Mr Bumble visits Mr Brownlow and tells him Oliver is a villain. Brownlow forbids Oliver's name ever to be mentioned to him again.

COMMENTARY: Although Dickens opens this chapter by denying that it is a comic break from the tragic tale of Oliver's misfortunes, the return to Oliver's home town does afford him the chance to reintroduce Bumble, again at Mrs Manning's garden gate. Comedy mixes freely with sentiment as Dickens caricatures the parochial world of half-starved children and brutal, unctuous officials. Dick is brought before Bumble. The little boy feels that he is dying and asks to be allowed to write a note for Oliver, full of tender love. This request gets him harsh words and a stay in the coal cellar.

Sadly for Oliver, a trip Bumble takes to London occasions his seeing in a newspaper Mr Brownlow's advertisement of a reward for information about Oliver. He rushes off to Brownlow's house, and there defames Oliver to Brownlow and his friend Grimwig. Brownlow believes it all and forbids anyone to mention Oliver to him again.

The reader sees how easily poor Oliver's reputation is dissolved by the acid of careless, pretentious speech. Bumble often seems funny, but the reader is never entirely allowed to lose sight of the harm he does to the unoffending children he supervises. Dickens's hatred of respectable preening is never more evident. His characters with moral worth are seldom shrewd, and can be disheartened and deceived by cunning people with quick tongues.

NOTES AND GLOSSARY:

seneschal: a medieval lord's chief servant

jackanapes: a conceited or impudent fellow, probably from 'Jack of Naples', a kind of monkey

demogalized: Mr Bumble's unique combination of demagogue, demogorgon and mogul, all words referring to people of almost supernatural power

Chapter 18: How Oliver passed his Time, in the improving Society of his reputable Friends

After being threatened by Fagin, Oliver is left alone for some weeks. Then the Dodger and Bates spend some time trying to persuade him to thieve. He meets a more agreeable thief, Tom Chitling, and watches as Fagin exerts himself to be amusing.

COMMENTARY: Oliver's isolation becomes intense. After some weeks of utter loneliness, he is allowed by the Dodger to clean his boots, and gratefully grasps at any chance of comradeship. The Dodger and Bates suggest that he should join the gang, offering him all its false friendships. Oliver gently declines. The reader cannot see how Oliver will survive without becoming a thief, and so poor Dick's fate seems to be closing on Oliver too.

Fagin enters with a youngster newly released from prison, another cheerful fellow like the Dodger and Charley Bates. They all drink together, along with Nancy's friend Betsy, until they become sleepy. It is the beginning of Oliver's real temptation, for after that he is constantly put with Charley Bates and the Dodger, and every day Fagin and they tell him stories so comic he cannot help but laugh, and prefer their company to the deadly solitude that is his sole alternative. Oliver's strength of character can be shown only by his resistance to becoming a thief. He cannot develop naturally.

NOTES AND GLOSSARY:
the regimentals: slang for prison uniform

Chapter 19: In which a notable Plan is discussed and determined on

Fagin visits Bill to discuss plans for a housebreaking. In Nancy's hearing, Fagin suggests that Oliver should accompany Bill. Bill intimates that he would kill Oliver if he blundered on the job. The robbery is planned for two nights later. Oliver is to be brought to Sikes by Nancy.

COMMENTARY: Fagin makes his way to Bill Sikes's flat in the dead of night, to plan a robbery with the housebreaker. He finds Sikes with Nancy. His fear of her shows a little, but she brushes it off and seems as prepared to stick to the low life as ever. Reassured, Fagin proceeds to talk over the robbery's details with Bill. It is decided to use Oliver, as his tiny size will make it easy to get him through a broken panel or small open window. Once in, he could let in the others. Sikes warns Fagin that he will kill Oliver if the boy gives him trouble. Nancy remains silent, but seems unmoved. They plan that she will collect Oliver from Fagin's den the next night, and bring him to Bill. Fagin returns home, delighted with the prospect of inveigling Oliver once and for all into the gang of thieves. Dickens shows him taking a perverse pleasure in ruining Oliver that marks him out as thoroughly evil. Even Nancy and Bill dislike and mistrust him. Fagin is utterly devoid of any human attachments.

NOTES AND GLOSSARY:
plate: objects made of silver
canary: yellow

Chapter 20: Wherein Oliver is delivered over to Mr William Sikes

Oliver is left by Fagin, in a dim room, with only a book about crimes, until Nancy arrives. She weeps over his innocence. Oliver thinks of escape, but she pleads with him to bide his time. She promises to help him another time if she can.

COMMENTARY: Oliver's luck seems to have run out altogether. Fagin prepares him for the night by giving him new shoes, and a book to read, in which famous crimes and trials are recounted. This well-thumbed volume has the opposite effect from that which Fagin intends. Oliver weeps and prays for deliverance. He is just finishing his plea, when Nancy disturbs him. She is distraught, stirred by a real compassion for him of a force which catches her off-guard. But she composes herself and shows Oliver the bruises she has suffered protecting him. She tells him that he must keep silent and help Bill for her sake. Now Oliver is truly in a dilemma. Someone is appealing to his compassion. If he refuses, he is heartless. If he complies, he is lost.

The reader follows the pair through the dark streets to Bill's lodgings. Bill threatens Oliver with a pistol, saying he will kill him if he gives trouble. Then he forces the boy to take a drink that will put him to sleep. Bill eats heartily, and goes to sleep, untroubled by the next day's plans. Nancy remains watching the fire, commissioned to wake them at five o'clock. She does not speak to Oliver, but moodily sits alone and silent.

Over and over, Dickens creates the suffocating darkness of utter loneliness around each character. The false camaraderie of the thieves and the brutish passion of Bill for Nancy give no comfort to Nancy's or Oliver's need for love. Yet the respectable world, where love is made possible by greater security, has no room for them. Its doors are shut to them. Dickens shows how Oliver and Nancy begin to feel love for each other, yet that love is threatened at every turn by violence and evil. Its very existence is a threat to their survival, weakening the self-interest with which they might guard against danger and violence. Dickens is at his least sentimental as Oliver goes off with Bill, with one last glance at Nancy, who does not look up from the fire.

NOTES AND GLOSSARY:

quail: tremble

Chapter 21: The Expedition

This chapter follows the lonely expedition of Oliver and Sikes out of London. After a full day's travel, they reach a decaying house.

COMMENTARY: This chapter opens by evoking the city in early morning hours. Oliver and Bill pass through the early mists from the suburbs into the busy Smithfield market as the day really comes to life. In the market place even the housebreaker is greeted by friends who offer the chance of a civil early morning drink. Awakened, the city contains all sorts of lives. Bill and Oliver pass on, and get a lift from a cart-driver, to the remote outskirts beyond Brentford, where gentlemen's houses enjoy a more secluded splendour. They loiter in the fields for some hours and then take dinner in a pub. There Sikes cadges them a lift to Shepperton, and in the dark evening hours, they are jostling along in another cart. As they travel, Oliver's weary mind begins to be oppressed by fear and gloom.

The trees seem to gesture and rustle in some grim joy that accepts the great night of cold death. When they dismount, Oliver fears Sikes will murder him. They cross over a bridge, and Oliver imagines dark water closing over him, but instead he is brought to a ruined house, its skeletal walls standing as a fearful reminder that all life passes. They enter.

This chapter creates the fearful atmosphere of crime. All around Sikes hovers this foul breath of menace. The reader knows now that Sikes is a man capable of murder, and fears for young Oliver's life.

NOTES AND GLOSSARY:

hawker:	street-seller
smock-frocks:	long, loose-fitting shirts worn in country districts
hostler:	one who takes care of horses at an inn or stable

Chapter 22: The Burglary

Oliver experiences his own unwitting involvement in crime, through a haze of terror. During the housebreaking, he is shot. Sikes drags him away.

COMMENTARY: A voice reaches them from inside the house. The burglar who has called out roughly wakens his own servant, Barney, to attend them. The characters seem almost safe again, back in the world of Fagin where status and rank matter as much as in the world of business. Toby Crackit, the more important housebreaker, is a fancy dresser and a cheerful drinker. He is amazed to be informed of the extent of Oliver's innocence, and insists the boy join them in a toast to the night's venture. Stupefied by weariness, drink and fear, Oliver dozes. Even when wakened, he keeps his innocence, seemingly only half-conscious of the crime to be committed. In the trusting gesture of all childhood, he puts his hand into Bill Sikes's as they go out. The reader is never allowed to forget that Oliver is only a little boy, vulnerable and inexperienced.

Bill, Toby, and Oliver walk through the cold and foggy night to a large house outside Chertsey. When they come to its garden wall, Dickens allows Oliver a moment of comprehension. He begs, in an oratory of innocent horror, to be allowed to 'die in the fields' rather than to be 'made to steal'. The burglars reply with oaths and threats. They drag him to the house, and push him through a little window. In one of Dickens's unforgettable touches, Crackit speaks of other boys carrying on in the same way 'for a moment or two, on a cold night'.

When Oliver enters the house he still hopes to rush upstairs and alert the family, despite Sikes's threats. However, they are roused by noise, and shout at him from the stairtop. Someone fires at him. Wounded, he returns to the window; Sikes pulls him through, and drags him away, but as the chapter closes, Oliver loses consciousness.

For a second time Oliver, the innocent accomplice, will be left to take the punishment for theft. For a second time, he passes, while unconscious, from the world of the criminals to the middle-class world of safety and comfort. The connections between these worlds are so rare, and often so vicious, that Dickens can contrive a way for Oliver to pass from one to the other only by strange and unusual means.

NOTES AND GLOSSARY:

glim:	(*slang*) light (from glimmer)
boot-jack:	a V-shaped device for use in pulling off boots
laudanum:	a draught containing opium
mug:	slang for face
imprecations:	curses

Chapter 23: Which contains the Substance of a pleasant Conversation between Mr Bumble and a Lady; and shows that even a Beadle may be susceptible on some points

---

While the reader wonders what is happening to Oliver, Dickens distracts him by relating Mr Bumble's courtship of Mrs Corney, on the same night. At a crucial moment, Mrs Corney is called away to hear the dying words of a pauper. With ill grace, she struts out.

COMMENTARY: Dickens again evokes the night-time of the city, with a vision of its outcasts shivering in the cold dark, some of them never to see daylight again, and deserving of pity 'whatever their crimes'. This is the confraternity in which Oliver suffers, and loses consciousness, though in his mind more than in many of theirs, there is a dim apprehension of another way of life. Between the outcasts and the comfortable, well-lit life is the officious grey land of public good works, represented in this chapter by Mr Bumble and Mrs Corney, while taking tea together in a workhouse. The scenes are comic, but they are played against the shadowy figures of the suffering, destitute inmates.

Corney and Bumble are an alliance of knowledge that the poor will be importunate unless deeply discouraged. They take tea in an island of respectable, warm comfort in the workhouse. Bumble's thoughts turn to wooing, and in a scene close to farce, he makes advances to the matron. Unfortunately, the courting is interrupted. An aged pauper respectfully intrudes to ask the matron to attend a dying woman, who must speak of something troubling her.

While she is out, Bumble greedily surveys Mrs Corney's few possessions, and settles his mind on matrimony.

NOTES AND GLOSSARY:

owdacious:	a mispronunciation for 'audacious', bold
efficacy:	effectiveness

Chapter 24: Treats of a very poor Subject. But is a short one; and may be found of Importance in this History

Mrs Corney attends the pauper's death, and hears the poor old woman's guilty secret. She had stolen something gold from a woman dying in childbirth. The child, when delivered, had been named Oliver.

COMMENTARY: This short chapter is crucial to the plot, for it contains a revelation about Oliver's birth. While Oliver lies half-dead, and unconscious, the reader hears of his hard beginning.

The dying woman is being carelessly attended by a young apothecary's assistant, in a cold garret. She is watched over by another old woman, and now by the pauper who went for Mrs Corney, and that good lady herself. The watcher says the dying woman couldn't take a mug of hot wine, so she drank it herself. Degrading poverty and callousness make the scene ghastly. The matron becomes angry at being kept waiting for the pauper's death and is ready to flounce out when a cry from the bed brings her back. The dying woman grabs her and asks that the others go. She confides that she nursed a young woman who died giving birth to a boy, and that she robbed her of something gold around her neck. The woman had told her her boy's heritage was no real disgrace. His name was Oliver. The matron bends forward eagerly to hear about the gold, but the old pauper dies, and the matron seems to leave disappointed as other old women come in to lay out their crony's body. Oliver's honourable heritage seems irretrievably lost, between the greedy grasping of the poor, and the selfish indifference of those who care for them. His innocence shines like a star, over a garbage dump.

NOTES AND GLOSSARY:

chidings:	scoldings
apothecary:	one who prepares and sells compounds for medical uses
harridans:	hags

Chapter 25: Wherein this History reverts to Mr Fagin and Company

Fagin waits anxiously for news of the housebreakers. Toby Crackit arrives, but cannot tell him where Sikes is, or whether Oliver is alive or dead.

COMMENTARY: The scene changes again, and the reader sees Fagin sitting in his own den, with his favourite boys behind him cheating Tom Chitling at cards. Chitling, just released from prison, is duped into revealing his warm feelings for Betsy, whom he protected by keeping quiet about her guilt in the theft. The others laugh at his feelings, angering him, until Fagin has to appeal for calm. Luckily the bell rings, and the company admits Toby Crackit. The boys disperse except for Dodger, who provides Crackit with a rough meal. Fagin watches anxiously as he eats. Even under such stress, each robber thinks only of himself.

Satisfied at last, Crackit dismays Fagin by asking about Bill Sikes. Both then become alarmed as neither knows his whereabouts or Oliver's. Crackit admits the robbery attempt failed, a fact Fagin already knew from the newspapers. He cannot enlighten Fagin (or the reader) about Oliver's fate, except to say they left him half-dead in a ditch. Fagin yelps with frustration. He has come to covet Oliver's soul.

NOTES AND GLOSSARY:

dummy: in the game of whist, the exposed fourth hand of cards, played by the player opposite, the dummy's partner

intimation: hint

Chapter 26: In which a mysterious Character appears upon the Scene; and many Things, inseparable from this History, are done and performed

---

Fagin goes to a criminal haunt, 'The Three Cripples' public house, looking for Bill Sikes. He also asks for Monks, but will not wait for him. Then he goes to Bill's lodgings, but finds only Nancy. Exasperated, he reveals his designs on Oliver. Nancy seems too drunk to understand him. At his own door, Fagin meets Monks. They discuss Oliver until Monks is disturbed by what he believes is a woman's shadow on the wall of the room.

COMMENTARY: Fagin hurries out, passing through the back streets where 'second-hand' handkerchiefs flutter at stalls like the flags of the underground society of pickpockets and thieves. Here Fagin is often greeted with a glance of recognition. But, in his own peculiar fashion, Fagin is hunting someone. He goes to a low public house, a dark place full of people who are degraded as well as poor. He asks the landlord furtively if 'he' is here, referring to Monks, a character unknown to the reader as yet.

Then Fagin proceeds to Bill's rooms to question Nancy about Sikes. Nancy is drunk, and comprehends little of Fagin's speech even when he has a terrible outburst of frustration, in which he cries that Oliver is worth hundreds of pounds to him, because of something chance threw his way, but that to get the money he is bound 'to a born devil'. Images of dark evil closing in on Fagin give the chapter almost the quality of a symbolic journey, through his familiar streets and yet deeper into the personal darkness of crime.

His final encounter is with Monks, who is waiting for him outside his own rooms. They go in together and the door closes in the darkness. They are afraid, even of each other. They have a private conversation about the transaction in Fagin's rooms and the reader learns Monks wants Oliver turned to crime, but not killed. Fagin would prefer that, but is less squeamish. Monks starts at the sight of a woman's shadow. They search, and find no one; both are convinced it was a figment of imagination, especially as Fagin announces he had locked the boys in their room. They part.

NOTES AND GLOSSARY:

intelligence: here, news, information
emporium: market place
denizens: inhabitants
cabriolet: a one-horse carriage

Chapter 27: Atones for the Unpoliteness of a former Chapter; which deserted a Lady, most unceremoniously

---

Mr Bumble decides on matrimony and requests Mrs Corney's hand. She consents. Bumble goes to Sowerberry's but finds only Noah Claypole, regaling himself with oysters and liquor, and Charlotte. They are courting, but Mr Bumble puts a stop to it.

COMMENTARY: Dickens now breaks away from Fagin's affairs to remind the reader of Oliver's other fearful oppressors, the calculating lower-middle-class people whose possessions and status determine to an exact degree their respectable place in society. He portrays them in a kind of savage comedy. Mr Bumble is wooing the workhouse matron Mrs Corney, whose nature is as self-seeking as his own. She comes in after attending the dying pauper, all a-flutter, and is handsomely revived by Mr Bumble with her own liquor. He then finishes off the cup. This leads to a romantic exchange ending in Bumble's outburst, 'Coals, candles, and house-rent free . . . . Oh, Mrs Corney, what an Angel you are!'. Mrs Corney evades his questions about the cause of her fright, deceitful and greedy even at such a moment.

Dickens reserves his most savage satire for people of this class and type. He treats criminals like Fagin in a more complex and deeper way. Perhaps because he had risen from this kind of background himself, he shows little pity for those clinging to respectable position. His young characters have more to fear from them than from anyone else. Critics often remark on the childlike intensity of Dickens's impressions. This is one instance in which childhood fears preclude a more mature compassion.

Bumble stops at Sowerberry's to order a coffin for the deceased pauper. Sowerberry is out but Noah Claypole and Charlotte are courting in the back parlour. Bumble is outraged, although he has just been involved in a little of that activity himself.

NOTES AND GLOSSARY:
waggish: sportive
acerbity: sharpness
acquiesced: agreed

Chapter 28: Looks after Oliver, and proceeds with his Adventures

---

Oliver rouses himself, and finds he is alone and wounded. He goes to the nearest house, the very house nearly robbed. There he knocks, and is roughly admitted by the servants. A young woman calls down instructions to carry him carefully upstairs.

COMMENTARY: This chapter reveals what became of Oliver Twist on that dreadful night when Sikes and Crackit forced him to join them in robbery. The robbers, surprised, were pursued by two not very brave menservants of the house, and an old tinker who had been sleeping in the shed. Fear overtook the burglars before the servants did, and they dropped Oliver in a ditch and fled. The men, too, became afraid, and returned to the house. Oliver lay unconscious until morning and then dragged himself up to the house, just managing to knock. When he was admitted a gentle young woman gave orders that he be brought upstairs while someone fetched a doctor and a constable.

The natural amiability of the servants and the gentle good nature of the girl contrast with the harshness of the relations among the thieves, and the cold calculation of Mr Bumble and Mrs Corney. Oliver has slipped, unconsciously, back into a world of goodness and good manners which is his natural milieu.

NOTES AND GLOSSARY:
affability: pleasantness
unmitigated: unrelieved

Chapter 29: Has an introductory Account of the Inmates of the House to which Oliver resorted

---

An old woman, the mistress of the house, and a young one, wait for the doctor and the constable. The doctor arrives, and attends the patient. Then he asks the ladies to accompany him upstairs.

COMMENTARY: This chapter introduces the reader to the ladies in the house, and to their close friend, Dr Losberne. It brings the reader up to date about developments in Oliver's situation, and shows him again happy and at peace in the affectionate, peaceful atmosphere where goodness, love and security prevail.

The house's mistress is a pleasant, alert old woman named Mrs Maylie. She has with her a girl of sixteen or seventeen named Rose. The girl's very name suggests the sweetness of her young nature. She is intelligent but simple in her goodness, representing the sort of angel of the fireside whom Dickens longed for, as an ideal woman. Their friend Dr Losberne is the local doctor, an eccentric, excitable bachelor, with a naturally warm heart. He arrives, flustered about their ordeal, and after attending their patient, asks them to come up and see the captured thief.

NOTES AND GLOSSARY:

gig: a light, two-wheeled, one-horse carriage

Chapter 30: Relates what Oliver's new Visitors thought of him

The sleeping Oliver is shown to Rose and Mrs Maylie, who are appalled at his youth. When he wakens he tells them his history. To protect Oliver, Dr Losberne presses the servants about their certainty that the boy is a thief, and they give way. However, at the last moment, London policemen arrive.

COMMENTARY: This scene ends in near-comedy although the whisperings of death are around it. Oliver arouses the deep compassion of the two women, and they and the doctor agree to hear his history before turning him over to the law. That evening Oliver tells them his pitiful story and they decide to protect him as well as they can. However, this requires a plan. Dr Losberne decides he must convince the menservants and the constable that Oliver is not the same boy as the one spotted with the thieves, but rather some beggar who arrived next morning at their door, in a woeful condition. He all but manages this, when his flow of speech is interrupted by the arrival of the Bow Street Runners, special London policemen sent for by the servants.

NOTES AND GLOSSARY:
loquacious: long-winded, wordy
stipulation: stated condition for agreement

Chapter 31: Involves a critical Position

The Bow Street policemen investigate, and report that the robbers were experts. They see Oliver, and, under the doctor's guidance, gradually conclude he had nothing to do with the crime.

COMMENTARY: The policemen Blathers and Duff are sharp-eyed, but pretentious. They manage to conclude that the thieves were professionals from the city, helped by a boy they put through a window. But the doctor's suggestions that Oliver is a boy shot by a spring-gun while trespassing on a neighbour's land confuse them and everyone else except the two women and Oliver himself, who knows nothing of his benefactors' efforts. The butler Giles is almost grateful when the doctor produces the gun and shows it to be unloaded, as his conscience is striken at the thought of nearly killing a child. Blathers and Duff hear of two men and a boy apprehended nearby for sleeping in a haystack, and this adds to their general impression that the thieves' young accomplice went away with his seniors in the trade. Oliver is left in peace, to recover.

NOTES AND GLOSSARY:

blunderbuss: a short firearm, with a large bore and a wide muzzle capable of holding several balls

---

Chapter 32: Of the happy Life Oliver began to lead with his kind Friends

Oliver and the doctor go to London to see Mr Brownlow. It is a day of double disappointment. On the way, Oliver espies the house where he was held prisoner, but when the doctor demands entry, the house and its occupant do not correspond to Oliver's description. The Brownlow house is vacant. Shortly thereafter the Maylie household goes to the country. Three happy months pass.

COMMENTARY: For a second time Oliver begins a happy life, in good company. He recovers slowly, and is brought by the Maylies to a country cottage. There he lives the relatively carefree life of a child on holiday. However, these days are preceded by one bitter disappointment. Dr Losberne and Oliver journey up to London to find Mr Brownlow and his household, but Mr Brownlow's house is to let. A neighbour says he has gone to the West Indies. Oliver nearly faints with disappointment. The chapter relates another strange incident. Before arriving at Mr Brownlow's, Oliver identifies a house as the one to which the thieves brought him. The good doctor jumps out, and demands entrance, only to find it solely occupied by a hump-backed and understandably bad-tempered little man; he also cannot help noticing that its interior furnishings do not answer to Oliver's description.

Despite this day, Oliver's spring passes happily. In such peaceful surroundings he finds he often thinks of his mother. His natural tenderness begins to develop, and if he seems a very little boy, he seems a promising one. He studies reading and writing and begins to enjoy the privileges of a protected childhood.

NOTES AND GLOSSARY:

corroborative: supporting or confirming

Chapter 33: Wherein the Happiness of Oliver and his Friends experiences a sudden Check

One summer evening Rose becomes ill. Oliver brings a letter summoning Dr Losberne to the nearest market-town for dispatch. Leaving the inn-yard he is menaced by a strange man; the man suffers a fit, and Oliver leaves before he recovers. Rose's condition worsens until it reaches a crisis. Dr Losberne arrives, and watches her through the crisis. She begins to recover.

COMMENTARY: As summer comes Oliver is flourishing, like the young plants and the fledgling birds he loves. The time seems to be set fair to pass happily when one night Rose Maylie suddenly becomes gravely ill. Dr Losberne is sent for in a letter which Oliver carries four miles to the nearest market-town. Mrs Maylie also gives him a second letter, addressed to Harry Maylie, Esquire, at 'some great lord's house in the country', but at the last moment she takes it back.

After dispatching the letter, Oliver is accosted by a madman who viciously threatens him before falling into a fit. Oliver gets help, but his mind is troubled as he leaves, for the man seemed to recognise him.

When he reaches the cottage, he forgets the encounter, in his terrible anxiety for Rose. She lies near death for some days. Oliver can scarcely believe death threatens her, surrounded as she is by love and beauty, and full of love and beauty herself. She falls into a deep sleep and passes the crisis of her illness.

Critics have often suggested that this incident is included merely because Dickens had recently lost his beloved sister-in-law, Mary Hogarth. Nevertheless, it brings home to Oliver, and so to the reader, the realisation that no one is safe from danger, however tranquil and pleasant his life may seem. This theme is continued in the next chapter, which discloses a secret suffering endured by Rose.

NOTES AND GLOSSARY:
affected: here, pretended
remonstrate: urge in opposition

Chapter 34: Contains some introductory Particulars relative to a young Gentleman who now arrives upon the Scene; and a new Adventure which happened to Oliver

When Oliver goes out for a ramble, he is stopped by two gentlemen in a carriage. He recognises Giles, and soon learns the other is Harry Maylie. Both seem deeply attached to Rose . On arriving at the house, Harry avows his love for Rose to his mother, but it clear she has doubts about it, and mentions a stain on Rose's name. Despite this, Harry determines to press his suit. One evening during Rose's recovery, Oliver is dozing, when he is disturbed by the strong impression that Fagin is near him. He wakens to see him at the window, with the madman from the inn-yard. They recognise him, and he calls for help.

COMMENTARY: The reader is introduced to Harry Maylie, Mrs Maylie's son, when he comes speeding down the road in a post-chaise, accompanied by the faithful Giles. The young man's concern for Rose immediately suggests a deep attachment to her. This is confirmed when Harry avows his love for Rose to his mother, and anxiously asks for her approval. She does not give it, because of 'a stain' on Rose's name, her 'doubtful birth', which may later cause Harry to regret his involvement. Harry remains with them, as Rose gradually recovers.

Then one evening, Oliver is dozing over his schoolbooks when through his sleep he senses the malicious presence of Fagin and a second man, even more full of hate. He wakes at the murmur of their voices, and seems to see them, just outside his window. The second man he recognises as the madman who had attacked him in the inn-yard. He calls for help. The beauty and peace of Oliver's new surroundings cannot give him, any more than Rose, real solutions to real dangers.

Chapter 35: Containing the unsatisfactory Result of Oliver's Adventure; and a Conversation of some Importance between Harry Maylie and Rose

---

Oliver and his friends give chase, but find no sign of the two intruders. After making many inquiries, they abandon the effort to trace them. Meanwhile Rose recovers her good health. Harry Maylie tells her of his love. She sadly sends him away, fearing that marriage to her would blight all his prospects. Harry asks for her permission to speak to her of marriage one more time, and receives it.

COMMENTARY: Oliver, Giles, Harry and the good doctor all give chase, but find no one, and no trace of anyone. They search for some time and make inquiries in the town, but no one sees anything of the two wicked men. Like two dark phantoms, they seem to vanish.

A few days later Rose is nearly well, and Harry speaks ardently to her of his love. She gently refuses him, speaking of this sad refusal as a duty. Her name is blighted; she will prevent his rise in the world if she accepts his proposal of marriage. Rose's real identity is unknown to her, but she knows her mother was unmarried. She was taken in as a child by Mrs Maylie, and feels she must repay that kindness by refusing to accept Harry. Pressed, she admits she deeply loves Harry. Harry asks if she would have accepted him if his prospects had been humbler, and she admits she would have, in a flood of tears. He gains one final promise from her, that she will listen to his suit once more, within a year. Then they part.

In this chapter the reader sees how unsentimental Dickens can be. The bourgeois world has its own coldness, its own rigid social rules. Harry and Rose find their mutual love is unacceptable, even to the good Mrs Maylie. Women of an age to be involved in romance are often portrayed by Dickens as social victims. Their natural goodness is no protection against the prejudice or evil of others. They do not rebel against this in any effective way. In this chapter Rose's situation manifests similarities to Oliver's. In a darker chapter, the reader will also see that her suffering opens her sympathies to Nancy.

NOTES AND GLOSSARY:
covert: hidden
insensible: unaware

Chapter 36: Is a very short one, and may appear of no great Importance in its Place. But it sould be read notwithstanding, as a Sequel to the last, and a Key to one that will follow when its Time arrives

Harry leaves, after asking Oliver to be his regular correspondent. Unseen, Rose watches him go.

COMMENTARY: This brief chapter tells of Harry's departure, after his interview with Rose. He seems deeply disturbed, and confides in no one. However, he asks Oliver to write to him once a fortnight saying how Rose and his mother are faring. This secret commission delights Oliver. Then Harry leaves for London, with Dr Losberne, as Rose watches sadly from an upstairs window.

NOTES AND GLOSSARY:

postillion: one who rides, as a guide, the near horse of one of
                     the pairs attached to a coach

Chapter 37: In which the Reader may perceive a Contrast, not uncommon in matrimonial Cases

Mr and Mrs Bumble contend for mastery. Mr Bumble loses, and retreats. In a public house, he encounters a suspicious stranger, who quizzes him about the birth of Oliver Twist, in return for money. They strike a bargain: Bumble will bring his wife the next night, and she will tell all she knows in return for more money.

COMMENTARY: The downfall of Mr Bumble is the subject of this chapter. He has fallen low in his own estimation since his marriage. He is mercilessly ordered about by his wife, who remains the one really in charge of the workhouse, although he is called its master. Bumble quarrels with his wife over who is to have mastery. She routs him completely because, as Dickens says, he is not just a bully but a coward. Bumble leaves the workhouse, and walks broodingly into a public house. There a dark stranger, almost an image of the devil himself, waits to tempt him.

The man gives Bumble money for information about Oliver's birth, and for the promise of more, Bumble agrees to bring Mrs Bumble to meet him, to tell him of the old pauper's revelations. As the chapter closes the reader learns this man is Monks, the mysterious figure who has pursued Oliver with hatred both to Fagin's den and to Mrs Maylie's country cottage. Menace stalks Oliver, dark shadows conceal his future.

NOTES AND GLOSSARY:

prerogative: exclusive privilege
relict: widow
murrain: plague

Chapter 38: Containing an Account of what passed between Mr and Mrs Bumble, and Mr Monks, at their nocturnal Interview

---

The Bumbles meet Monks at a tumbledown warehouse. For twenty-five pounds, Mrs Bumble reveals that the old pauper died clutching a pawn ticket, which she redeemed. Monks is satisfied, when she gives him the redeemed items. As they watch, he raises a trap-door over an old watermill, and drops those tokens of Oliver's true identity into the churning water below.

COMMENTARY: On an overcast summer evening, Bumble leads Mrs Bumble to a miserable, vacant factory, a place of faceless decay. There they meet Monks, just as a thunderstorm breaks. Again he seems to come from hell itself. He is an unreal character whose personality is a distortion of human nature. Mrs Bumble hopes to trick him in some way, but he easily dominates her. He invites her to crime, with such menace that the reader wonders why the Bumbles do not flee, but they follow him to the attic of the building and there the three sit in conference. Mrs Bumble bargains mercilessly with Monks. She receives twenty-five pounds for her secret knowledge. But she gives Monks more than that; she gives him a small kid bag with a gold locket, and a plain gold wedding-ring engraved with the name 'Agnes'. There is no surname, but there is a date, within the year before Oliver's birth. Monks is satisfied. He opens a trap-door that is over a wrecked watermill. Speaking recklessly of how he might have murdered them, he throws the bag and its contents into the turbulent water. Then they all breathe more easily. Monks shows them out. Fearful of being alone, he calls to a boy to light his way back up to the attic. A lost soul, he knows his own evil.

NOTES AND GLOSSARY:

paltry:	worthless
feint:	a mock attack
facetiousness:	jocular humour

Chapter 39: Introduces some respectable Characters with whom the Reader is already acquainted, and shows how Monks and the Jew laid their worthy Heads together

---

The reader now looks in on Sikes, who is wasted with illness, and in poorer lodgings than previously. Nancy has nursed him and Fagin is visiting him. Bill demands money. They agree that Nancy will go back with Fagin to collect it. Money has not yet changed hands at Fagin's when Monks arrives and, in Nancy's hearing, speaks with the old Jew. Nancy leaves quietly but, when she is out of sight, runs away in great distress. The next day she goes to a quiet, respectable hotel in the smarter part of London, and demands to see Rose Maylie.

COMMENTARY: in this chapter the reader rejoins the thieves. Sikes, reduced to poverty by illness, has recovered enough to be visited by Fagin and his lads. Nursed by Nancy, Bill is unable to show her any real gratitude or affection. He remains almost savage, even when she faints with weariness. When she recovers, Bill insists that she accompany Fagin back to his den, to collect some money.

Monks soon arrives at Fagin's, to tell Fagin something which Nancy makes it her business to overhear. They are unaware of her listening, and after Monks leaves, she collects the money and leaves quickly. But in the street she runs until she is exhausted, and bursts into tears. Then she runs back to Sikes's lodgings.

Late the next day, Nancy leaves the sleeping Sikes, in great agitation giving him a tender kiss before she goes. The reader senses that all her basic tenderness is awakened, and that she has resolved upon some desperate step. She runs a long distance into the wealthier part of town, where she goes to a hotel. There she asks for Miss Maylie, and with great difficulty persuades the staff to bring her message to Rose.

NOTES AND GLOSSARY:

abutting:	bordering
asperities:	harsh remarks
Dianas:	virgins, votaries of the chaste Greek goddess, Diana

Chapter 40: A strange Interview, which is a sequel to the last Chapter

Nancy reveals to Rose all she knows of Oliver's real history, including the plotting against him by Fagin and Monks. Despite Rose's entreaties, she leaves, promising only to walk on London Bridge each Sunday night, so that Rose may contact her again.

COMMENTARY: This chapter brings together two young women, both scarred by sorrow in love. One is respectable and pure, the other fallen and desperate. Yet both have a natural goodness that makes them form a bond of mutual care for Oliver. In fact Rose's kindness touches Nancy herself, and the girl weeps over her own life. She confesses to Rose that she abducted Oliver when he ran the message for Mr Brownlow, and warns Rose of Monks. She tells all she has heard: that Monks spotted Oliver with Fagin's boys, and that he struck an evil bargain with Fagin. They agreed Fagin would train the boy as a thief and then allow him to be captured and hanged. Thus, Monks schemed, he would get legal possession of Oliver's rightful inheritance, for he is Oliver's half-brother. He knows Oliver's real identity but all evidence of it is now destroyed. As Dickens unfolds all this, a new movement in the action seems to be astir. Oliver's secret parentage will be revealed.

The encounter between the two women is a spiritual melodrama in which the two women represent fallen and unfallen womanhood. Each is warmhearted, but one is weighed down by a terrible shame, and entangled in an unworthy love. Their speech is stilted, and highly charged with emotion. Nancy calls Rose 'lady' throughout the conversation, and often refers to 'such as me'. Despite this, the chapter reflects in certain ways the bitter social reality of the gulf between the poor, fallen London women and middle-class ladies; each can see the other only as a type. When Rose offers Nancy money, to enable her to lead an honest life, that gulf, between Rose's security and Nancy's total unease, is very vividly shown. With a vestige of pride and a terrible despair, Nancy refuses the money and leaves. As she goes, she promises to walk on London Bridge each Sunday night between eleven and midnight, so that Rose may easily find her again.

NOTES AND GLOSSARY:
obliterated: wiped out

Chapter 41: Containing fresh Discoveries, and showing that Surprises, like Misfortunes, seldom come alone

Oliver sees Mr Brownlow entering a house, and Giles gets him the address. With Rose, he goes to Brownlow's. Privately, Rose tells Mr Brownlow Nancy's story, and they with others plan how to help Oliver.

COMMENTARY: In sharp contrast to the previous chapter, this chapter shows Rose with those of her own kind; she and Oliver visit Mr Brownlow and Mr Grimwig whom Oliver had chanced to see entering a house. From Chapter 40 onwards, different threads of Oliver's life begin to be woven together, by the power of coincidence.

Nancy's story is fully told only to Mr Brownlow, but everyone in Rose's circle of friends hears enough to bond together into a committee to help Oliver to obtain his rightful inheritance. Harry Maylie is also going to be asked to help, a fact which Rose finds disturbing. Dickens gently suggests that her own difficulties may be nearer to resolution than she imagines. Like Oliver, she belongs ultimately to the safe and happy world which money and goodness combine to protect. They will both be taken in, rescued. This hope of individual rescues is the only one Dickens allows. It is held against a dark background of many miserable lives.

NOTES AND GLOSSARY:

flurried: agitated
hackney-coach: hired coach
despatch: dispatch, haste
nanikeen breeches and gaiters: yellow trousers of nankeen cloth, and cloth coverings for the ankles

---

Chapter 42: An old Acquaintance of Oliver's exhibiting decided Marks of Genius, becomes a public Character in the Metropolis

---

Noah and Charlotte have robbed the Sowerberrys and set out for London. They arrive at the Three Cripples, where Fagin takes an interest in them. They arrange an appointment with a friend of Fagin, who will help them enter a new line of work.

COMMENTARY: In this chapter yet another two figures from Oliver's past make their way into London. This great city attracts to itself all kinds of people with a great variety of purposes and plans. By bringing the characters to one place, Dickens gives the power of coincidence a chance to work. But incidentally he creates a dramatic impression of the living city, complex and fascinating.

Noah Claypole and Charlotte come to London to make an illegal fortune, and seek out the pub the Three Cripples, which is one of Fagin's haunts. He overhears them talking and, for payment of the twenty pounds Charlotte had stolen from the till at Sowerberry's, agrees to set them up. Noah plans light work for himself, stealing from children sent out on errands, and heavier work for Charlotte, in the pickpocketing line. Fagin admires his haughty ill-treatment of Charlotte, perhaps mentally wishing Sikes had as firm control over his Nancy. Indeed Noah and Charlotte are a more cunning, more stupid and unskilled pair than Sikes and Nancy, but they parallel them, and suggest that for every Nancy, who would seek a new life if she could bring herself to hope for it, there are several anxious for quick money and not fussy about its source. Yet the reader can feel a quick pang of pity for this seedy pair, who think themselves clever, as Fagin winds tentacles around them, and sucks away the first illegal twenty pounds they ever made.

NOTES AND GLOSSARY:

encumbered: burdened
reticule: a small bag
rapacity: greed

Chapter 43: Wherein is shown how the Artful Dodger got into Trouble

Noah and Charlotte keep the appointment with Fagin's 'friend', who is Fagin himself. In passing, he tells them the sad story of the Dodger's capture. Charley Bates, joining the discussion, is cheered only by the hope that the Dodger will have a memorable trial. Noah is sent to Bow Street to hear him committed.

COMMENTARY: Fagin shows his hand the next day when he warns Noah that the gallows can make him their victim, at a word from him. In giving Fagin the twenty pounds, Noah has given him material evidence of his past crime, and can be blackmailed if necessary. Noah's respect for Fagin grows, and his desire to join Fagin's band only increases.

Fagin relates the sad fate of his 'best hand', the Dodger, who was picked up with a stolen snuffbox on him. Charley Bates comes in, full of woe. The owner of the box is ready to testify, and the Dodger will get a sentence of 'transportation for life' to Australia. Bates feels the Dodger's position deeply. He must have hoped to go out on a note of great honour, a truly impressive crime. Fagin consoles him; the Dodger shall have a lawyer to defend him and a chance to speak from the dock. He shall have a fine hour.

Noah is forced to go off to the court, disguised, to watch the Dodger's first scene there. It is well worth seeing, as the Dodger airily threatens the magistrate and officers with legal suits, and says his attorney is breakfasting with the vice-president of the House of Commons. Bates waits outside for this cheering news.

NOTES AND GLOSSARY:

cravat: neck scarf, here slang for a noose, the hangman's rope
codger: old crank

Chapter 44: The Time arrives for Nancy to redeem her Pledge to Rose Maylie. She fails

---

Sunday night comes, but Nancy is kept in by Bill and Fagin, who uneasily sense that her mood of desperation is dangerous to them. Fagin misunderstands, and privately offers her the means of killing Bill. She does not accept, and so Fagin decides to have her shadowed.

COMMENTARY:

In this chapter, the crisis between Bill and Nancy begins to gather, like a dark cloud presaging a thunderstorm. Nancy and Bill are visited by Fagin. While he is there, Nancy decides she wants to go out, but Bill forcibly prevents her. The struggle between them is more serious, more pervaded by adult passions, than the contest between the Bumbles, or the easy conquest Noah had made of Charlotte. Adult passion involves deep issues of life and death, of the meaning of life, and this is the area of struggle between Bill and Nancy. They had had a bond of trust amid all the brutal mistrust of thieves toward one another. Nancy intends to be loyal to Bill, but almost against her will she is drawn to something else, to providing Oliver with a better life. The urge to mother the child is perhaps the only passion as deep in her as her regard for the housebreaker. She is driven to keep both trusts, but Bill will brook no second loyalty. Although the scenes may partake of the melodrama of stage 'low life', Nancy's problems are known to the hearts of many women who feel more than one commitment.

Fagin, like an evil father, attempts to pry into Nancy's heart, but her mystery is sealed to him. He sees enough to know she feels some other loyalty and, having no experience of loyalty, assumes this ends her relationship with Bill. He offers her the means of ridding herself of Bill, to be free for what he takes to be involvement with another man. If she accepts, he will be able to blackmail her with his knowledge of her crime. Nancy shows him so little of her mind that he goes away hopeful. However, to be sure of increasing his power over her, Fagin decides to have her followed.

NOTES AND GLOSSARY:

dissimulation: feigning

myrmidons: subordinates who execute orders with protest or pity

---

Chapter 45: Noah Claypole is employed by Fagin on a secret Mission

---

In this brief chapter, Noah Claypole is hired by Fagin to spy on Nancy. He follows her out of the Three Cripples.

COMMENTARY: The real sliminess of Fagin becomes apparent in this chapter as he connives with Noah to track down Nancy's new love. For six nights Noah waits, ready to follow Nancy. On the seventh night Fagin tells him she is going out to keep an appointment and, delighted with his new job, Noah trails her along the dark streets. Just as Chapters 40 and 41 showed Oliver's and Rose's fates becoming bright, this shows Nancy's becoming dark, doomed. The unhappy coincidence of Fagin's seeing her attempt to get out the week before was bad luck; Noah's successful trailing is much worse.

NOTES AND GLOSSARY:

goes abroad: here used in the old sense, goes out of doors

Chapter 46: The Appointment kept

Watched by the cunning eyes of Noah, Nancy meets Rose Maylie and Mr Brownlow on London Bridge. She refuses to betray Fagin, but tells them where they are likely to meet with Monks and how to recognise him. Brownlow is startled by the description; he thinks he knows the man. Despite offers of help, Nancy leaves them, taking only a handkerchief of Rose's as a memento.

COMMENTARY: A high pitch of drama is reached as Nancy goes to keep her appointment with Rose on London Bridge. The night itself seems ominous; the water is covered with a mist that catches the red glare of fires burnt on small craft for warmth. Much is hidden from sight, but Nancy cannot hide from Noah; Fagin's evil eye is upon her through his minion. As usual, Fagin does little himself, but makes others do his work.

Dickens prepares the reader for Rose's arrival with astonishing contrasts: 'Midnight had come upon the crowded city. The palace, the night-cellar, the jail, the madhouse: the chambers of birth and death, of health and sickness, the rigid face of the corpse and the calm sleep of the child: midnight was upon them all.' Rose arrives, protected by a gentleman. Nancy is in such fear she leads them down the steps of the bridge. Despite her own sense of foreboding, Nancy tells them where they may apprehend Monks and how to recognise him. Her description deeply startles Rose's companion, who seems to know the man. After that he speaks to Nancy of her future, and she tells him she will surely end as many do, by drowning herself. Rose offers her money, but, as she did the first time, she refuses. Helping Oliver is a precious experience for her. She asks only a memento from Rose. Rose and Brownlow leave in a carriage; Nancy and Noah make their ways back into the dark streets.

NOTES AND GLOSSARY:

importunate: urgently requesting
obdurate: hard-hearted

Chapter 47: Fatal Consequences

Fagin is enraged by Noah's report. When Sikes comes in, he shares the bitter news with him, and sets him loose to do his worst to Nancy. Sikes goes to his lodgings, wakens Nancy, and as she pleads with him, beats her to death.

COMMENTARY: The transformation of Fagin into a devil is nearly complete, as he sits brooding 'with face so distorted and pale, and eyes so red and bloodshot, that he looked less like a man, than like some hideous phantom, moist from the grave, and worried by an evil spirit'. He has already heard Noah's news – Dickens moves the novel along almost as a play moves, from scene to scene. Now Fagin waits for Sikes, whose savage nature will be as roused as his own.

What happens then is terrifying. Bill comes in, and Noah is wakened to tell again the disloyal acts and words of Nancy. Bill flares into a passionate rage and knowingly, almost gleefully, Fagin sends him out to murder her. Again Fagin himself does nothing; he incites evil, but always manages to avoid acting himself.

Bill breaks in upon Nancy as she sleeps. She pleads with him to run away with her to a better life, but he strikes her, and as she falls, she pleads with God for mercy. Rose's white handkerchief is covered with blood. This is the closest Rose will come to real sorrow and hopelessness.

Bill strikes her again with a club, and she is dead. Dickens refers to Bill then as 'the murderer'. One of his imaginative gifts is playing with the characters as people and as types, until the personality and its typical qualities seem to suffuse each other. The chapter closes as Sikes commits this horrible crime of brutal savagery.

NOTES AND GLOSSARY:
palter: act insincerely

Chapter 48: The Flight of Sikes

Sikes leaves his lodgings and goes outside the city. He stops at a pub, but is frightened away by a salesman who offers to clean his hat. He feels haunted by Nancy's ghost. As he tries to sleep, he hears shouts of alarm; he sees a fire and joins the local people in fighting it. After this, he decides to return to London. He is afraid to bring his dog with him, so he tries to drown it, but the animal runs away.

COMMENTARY: This chapter opens with the dreadful scene of the half-maddened Sikes staring at Nancy's gory corpse. Even in his shocked state, the housebreaker realises he must flee, and so begins another London walk which resonates in the reader's memory with Oliver's dreadful journey towards Mrs Maylie's house, and with other walks: Dodger and Oliver to Fagin's den; Noah and Charlotte to the Three Cripples, Fagin himself to the Three Cripples; poor Nancy first to Rose's hotel, and later to the bridge. For those who travel without the safety of a carriage each journey is fraught with dangers, and this is especially so for the criminal who fears recognition. However frightened he is, Sikes must eat, and he stops at a village pub. A salesman takes his hat to demonstrate a stain-remover, and Sikes, crazed, overturns a table and runs out. Dogged by a shadowy ghost of Nancy, he goes down a dark road. He tries sleeping in a wayside shed, but his fears are too great for real sleep. When he leaves the shed and sees a fire, the reader senses that the man has entered hell. But he fights the fire heroically. Sikes is no demon, just a lost soul. With great psychological accuracy, Dickens tells of the murderer's relief in the tremendous excitement of the fire and of his need afterwards to return to London. There his life will not be this terrible solitary flight. But Dickens raises the real question of whether it can be anything else, as Sikes tries to drown his dog and the beast takes flight.

NOTES AND GLOSSARY:

mountebank:	a quack salesman
composition:	mixture
loquacity:	talkativeness

Chapter 49: Monks and Mr Brownlow at length meet. Their Conversation, and the Intelligence that interrupts it

---

Monks has been apprehended by men hired by Brownlow. Monks and Brownlow privately discuss Monks's sordid life and his evil designs upon Oliver. Dr Losberne interrupts them with the news that Sikes and Fagin are about to be captured.

COMMENTARY: This is the necessary chapter in a melodramatic story, in which secrets are revealed and perplexing mysteries resolved. Through Nancy's help, Brownlow has captured Monks and forces him to a private confession of villainy. He is Oliver's half-brother, the older child of Mr Brownlow's best friend, Leeford, conceived in a loveless marriage ended with separation. Oliver is the love-child of Leeford's second union, and was by his will entitled to an inheritance. Monks, taking a new name, came across Oliver by chance, and then sought out any proofs of his identity; with the Bumbles' help he destroyed them, but Nancy's silent presence witnessed his re-telling of this to Fagin. With Fagin, Monks was in a dreadful bond to ruin Oliver. Nancy worked against this at almost every turn, but died for her efforts. Brownlow's efforts have been spurred on by the only passion of his life, his love for

Leeford's sister. She died years earlier, and in her honour, he remained a lifelong friend to her weaker brother. The brother had entrusted a portrait of his second love, Oliver's mother, to Brownlow, before a journey that was to end in illness and death. This portrait so resembled Oliver that Brownlow realised, when the waif first came under his protection, that he was their child. When he lost Oliver, he took up the trail of Monks, going to the West Indies where Monks had an estate. When he returned, his reunion with Oliver brought him into contact with Rose Maylie, and through her with Nancy. Coincidence, or the hand of heaven, thus directed events to Oliver's good.

This is the energetic pace of action which enlivens stage melodrama and keeps the audience in a shiver of emotions. Evil is undone by the greater power of good. Victims of evil already dead seem to assist the course of justice. Some innocence is wretchedly betrayed and lost. Other innocence is protected. In the end so much has happened that much explanation is required to enable the audience to grasp the many events of the plot in their true significance.

NOTES AND GLOSSARY:

impeach:	to charge with a crime
felon:	criminal
indemnified:	paid
maudlin:	sentimental and silly
attesting:	swearing to the truth of a statement

Chapter 50: The Pursuit and Escape

The scene changes to Jacob's Island, a waterside area of decaying warehouses and tenements. There Toby Crackit and Kags are brooding with Mr Chitling about the arrest of most of the gang. Sikes's dog bursts in. That night Sikes also arrives. A little later, Charley Bates also turns up. He attacks Sikes and calls out. A crowd gathers, eager to take Sikes, who tries to escape from the rooftop by means of a rope. He slips and is hanged.

COMMENTARY: This takes us away from Brownlow's study, where Monks is imprisoned, to another prison – the slum room where Mr Chitling and Toby Crackit are hiding with a criminal returned from Australia. The three discuss the terrible events of the day. Fagin has been captured, Bet has gone mad, the people at the Cripples are all in custody, and Noah Claypole (alias Bolter) is going to turn King's evidence, enabling the judge to order Fagin to be hanged. Sikes's dog then bounds in, terrifying them further. Sikes arrives, in a terrible condition. Bates also comes in, but is horrified at Sikes being there, and fights with him, all the while crying out, 'Murder!'. People hear the cry, and an angry crowd gathers.

Sikes hopes to escape by going out through the roof and dropping into the water, but the tide is out and the human tide swirls angrily beneath him. Sikes wants to make a desperate attempt to lower himself on a rope just as Brownlow's voice is heard in the crowd, but the ghost of Nancy causes him to start, and he drops down, hanged by his own rope. His dog leaps out after him, and falls to the ground. A more macabre end to a criminal life can scarcely be imagined. The reader is struck by the force with which the passion of the angry crowd clashes with Sikes's own dark passions, causing yet another death.

NOTES AND GLOSSARY:

colliers:	vessels for transporting coal
transport:	criminal sent to Australia, where the English ran a penal colony

Chapter 51: Affording an Explanation of more Mysteries than one, and comprehending a Proposal of Marriage with no Word of Settlement or Pin-money

The friends reunite in the town where Oliver was born. Rose and Oliver learn the truth of their identities, as Monks discloses all he knows before them and their assembled friends. Two old paupers, and the Bumbles, are brought in to confirm some details. Harry Maylie also arrives, and again offers his hand in marriage to Rose. He is now a country parson, so Rose gladly accepts him. Oliver discovers that his first friend, Dick, is dead.

COMMENTARY: More mysteries are explained in this chapter, a bitter-sweet chapter of disclosures that bring some joy and some grief. It is set in a comfortable hotel, in the town where Oliver was born. Going there, he passes Sowerberry's and the familiar workhouse; thus, the reader is once again reminded of the many poor children whose circumstances do not alter except for the worse.

Monks is brought to a gathering of Mr Grimwig, Mr Brownlow, Oliver, Rose, and Mrs Maylie. Before them all, at Mr Brownlow's insistence, he confirms that Oliver is his half-brother whom he has pursued with malice, so that he will end in poverty and disgrace. He also shocks the reader with the new admission that Rose is the young sister of Oliver's dead mother. After this revelation, Harry Maylie enters the room; poor Rose's hard-pressed feelings are further tested by his renewed suit. She nobly declines his offer of marriage, until he assures her that he has renounced bright political hopes for a country parsonage. Then she accepts him.

Comic relief is provided when the Bumbles are brought in to admit knowledge of the proofs of Oliver's identity. Forced to confess that they had sold the locket and ring to Monks, they face a bleak future. Mr Bumble retains just enough spirit to proclaim that if the law assumes a man directs his wife, it looks on with the eye of a bachelor. In the many feelings of this chapter, sorrow is the last, for Oliver learns that his oldest friend, Dick, has died without help or comfort of any kind.

NOTES AND GLOSSARY:
chinks: small cracks

Chapter 52: Fagin's Last Night alive

Fagin's trial ends in his being deemed guilty and sentenced to death. He awaits death, alone, frightened and confused. Into his solitude break Oliver and Mr Brownlow, to ask him about missing papers. He gives the information, hoping with their help to escape. But there is no escape.

COMMENTARY: The last days of Fagin's life are related in a spectacle of macabre gloom that begins in court and ends beside the gallows. Throughout the chapter, Dickens enters into the old criminal's thoughts, almost with gusto, encouraging the reader to understand the bewildered terror and rage that unbalance Fagin's mind. Fagin still gives an impression of attempted shrewdness, but is so dazed, and so trapped, that it seems only habit. He cannot repent. He can only dream of escape, even as he sits in the condemned cell.

Brownlow brings Oliver to see him, trying to find out from Fagin if any papers concerning Oliver were entrusted to him by Monks. Fagin actually tells Oliver where they are hidden, and in return wants Oliver to help him escape. Of course, there is no escape, and when the two worthy characters leave, the evil man is left to his own miserable fate.

NOTES AND GLOSSARY:
opprobrious: abusive
turnkey: a prison warder

Chapter 53: And Last

The concluding chapter tells the subsequent history of the book's main characters, pointing out the moral: only the good achieve real happiness, and they only through sacrifice and effort.

COMMENTARY: This final chapter relates the later fortunes of all the main characters. Rose and Harry marry, and with them in the vicarage lives old Mrs Maylie. Nearby live Oliver and Mr Brownlow. Mr Brownlow adopts Oliver and takes great pleasure in teaching him. Mr Losberne gives up medical practice and takes a cottage in the same village. He and Grimwig become fast friends. As the years pass this happy little group is also blessed by the addition of children, whose lively good-humour ensures that Rose will be very busy.

In contrast, the Bumbles live on in disgrace, ending in the workhouse. Fagin's gang disintegrates. Monks goes to America with his father's money, but dies there in prison. Only Charley Bates takes the warning from the events of the past, and turns to honest farming for a living.

Oliver's inheritance is modest but comfortable. Dickens's picture of happiness is often middle-class, for he fears the corrupting power of money.

The last remarks of the novel refer to Oliver's mother, the gentle ghost whose love has penetrated the atmosphere in which Oliver lives. Dickens suggests his respect for her, despite her being that most disgraced nineteenth-century figure, an unmarried mother.

NOTES AND GLOSSARY:

felicity: happiness
grazier: a man who keeps sheep

Part 3

Commentary

Oliver Twist is highly entertaining, and can be immediately enjoyed, but it repays close study. A reader can learn much about the writer's craft from Dickens, who creates scenes of sentiment, horror, or merriment with equal zest.

Themes

Oliver Twist is a complex novel, richly stocked with thoughtful impressions of various kinds of lives. It does not merely tell of 'the parish boy's progress', but leads the reader into the criminal underworld, and the comfortable and sedate world of the well-to-do. Because of this variety, the novel has no one simple theme, but certain recurring ideas persist in the reader's imagination long after he has closed the book.

Crime is linked with isolation

The initial impression of gay camaraderie among thieves is first corroded by the easy betrayal of Oliver to the police in Chapter 10. Thereafter almost every scene involving the criminals further suggests that the cheerful facade covers the terrible loneliness of their lives. Nancy's gruesome fate is not just her death, but the death of her hopes for love in such company. She gives a genuine regard to Bill Sikes, but his violent nature and easy mistrust of everyone betray her. He ends, as Fagin does, in a solitude akin to madness.

Some critics highlight the thieves setting up an alternative society, opposed to the basic social order of nineteenth-century England. Certainly the gang has a hierarchy, and divides up its labour. It does link its members in a loose camaraderie, and is some comfort against the hostility of the law. However, the credo of its most successful members is looking after self first, and others only as necessary. The boys in the gang do not quite understand this, but the adults do. The worst of them, Fagin, has no conscience about sending others to prison, transportation, or even the gallows. In fact, as Chapter 44 shows, he will arrange the death of an awkward member himself.

The deep isolation of this life withers the affections. Nancy has few feelings, and Monks and Fagin almost none. Their own regard even for themselves is an earnest effort to get as much money as possible, not a deeper urge to make something of themselves. They are almost caricatures of the essential shallowness of criminality.

This lack of life is what Oliver fears most. Like any child, he craves affection and attention. He needs it to develop a character and personality of his own. The reader senses Oliver's fear of spiritual extinction if he is forced to lead a life of crime. In Nancy Dickens shows the ravages of such a life on an intrinsically generous nature, and a last desperate struggle to express her maternal urge by a woman who has lost all hope of children.

Social order has its victims

The real sufferings of the poor and degraded scarcely touch the consciousness of the wealthy. Nineteenth-century English society was indeed unequally divided, with roughly only ten per cent living comfortable, protected lives, and the rest in a descending order of struggling tradesmen or craftsmen, skilled labour and servants, unskilled labour, migrating homeless labour, and the jobless poor. Mayhew estimated that among the labouring poor at any given time only one-third were fully employed, and another one-third partially employed. Despite the vast numbers of the poor, social consciousness proved slow to respond to need. Poor Laws, free schools, public health authorities, came about only slowly and grudgingly. Dickens caricatures the administrators of public good works without mercy, but he attempts to show the real need for the social order to widen its concerns beyond the protection of property and the maintenance of public order.

The dead influence the living

Throughout the story, the dead seem present in the minds of living characters, in such a way as to affect their actions. Mr Brownlow is deeply moved by Oliver's resemblance to his dead mother, and Oliver frequently senses her protecting love. Agnes also haunts the memory of the old pauper who robbed her corpse, and so the secret of Oliver's identity is kept and passed on to the Bumbles and Monks.

Oliver begins his own career among coffins, and loses his young friend Dick to an early death. He has lost both his mother and father in infancy, but he defends his mother's good name, at the cost of his position at Sowerberry's. He speaks of her when first at Mr Brownlow's and thus touches the heart of the old housekeeper.

In a different and darker vein, Sikes is dragged to his doom by the awful bond he has forged in blood with his lover Nancy. She is a ghostly presence in his last days, and the very means of his destruction. Pity for Nancy spurs Brownlow to hunt Monks down. His own lost friends

Edward Leeford, and Edward's sister, keep him loyal to Oliver, once he realises his identity.

In all this, death is imaginatively reckoned with, in a personal way that is rare in modern novels, and perhaps truer to life than current writing can be.

Plot and structure

The plot of this large novel is complicated and busy. Dickens shifts the scenes frequently and keeps alive the reader's double anxiety: will the forces of good reclaim Oliver; will the forces of evil suck him down? As in life, many people's stories seem to be overlapping, several are completely told by the novel's close:

(i) the progress of Oliver from parish boy, to near-crime, to happy middle-class life;

(ii) the romance of Rose and Harry Maylie, its problems and eventual resolution;

(iii) the less happy romance of Edward Leeford and Agnes, its end in sorrow and death, with Oliver as its living issue and only hope;

(iv) the inglorious history and eventual downfall of the evil corrupter of children, Fagin;

(v) Brownlow's early unhappy love, his loss of his trusted male friend, and his renewed hope and affection in his relation to Oliver, with its anxieties and tribulations, and eventual fulfilment;

(vi) Bumble's career, his romance, his temptation and fall, and his sad fate.

A lesser novelist could have made a small novel of any one of these. Dickens indeed had a mind teeming with plots.

He used the serial structure forced on him by writing for magazines, with much greater aplomb than most other nineteenth-century novelists. Dickens had no qualms about being a popular entertainer, and willingly expanded the role of popular characters or added unexpected turns to the plot if the letters received from readers suggested this was required. *Oliver Twist* was in a popular 'Newgate' tradition of crime novels, though it had an imaginative force that made it something greater. Perhaps Dickens's ease in writing instalments came from his lifelong love of the theatre. Nineteenth-century English theatre was poor, and often melodramatic, but its stock characters moved from one exciting scene to the next, leaving audiences gaping at their adventures. The theatricality of Dickens's writing made episodic writing more natural to him.

Coincidences abound in *Oliver Twist*. Fagin meets Monks by chance;

earlier, Monks encounters Bumble just when the other is in a talkative mood. Nancy and Sikes capture Oliver when he is on Mr Brownlow's errand because they chance to meet him in the street. Nancy overhears the name of Rose Maylie's hotel when she is unnoticed by Monks and Fagin. But it is not only the action which is moved along by coincidences; the deeper emotional relationships among the characters are affected by the chance that Oliver should encounter the one person who might care for Agnes's child, Mr Brownlow, and then become involved with Agnes's lost sister. Dickens risks making the book's emotional impact dependent on coincidences which are made only slightly more credible by the insertion of coincidences which fail to cause anything, that is, Oliver's spotting Fagin's den while out with Dr Losberne, and Oliver's waking to see Fagin and Monks at the window in Chapter 34.

Settings

London

Oliver Twist leaves the reader with an overwhelmingly vivid impression of the living, diverse, and crowded streets of London. Dickens was not the first writer to be drawn to writing about the city; Dr Johnson's famous dictum that a man who is tired of London is tired of life held for many minor writers, and several great illustrators, including Dickens's own collaborator George Cruikshank. The great contrast between rich and poor was inevitably noticed there, where genteel town houses and parks shouldered bad slums whose tenements could never quite house the vast influx of people from the countryside. This contrast is one of Dickens's themes. The real unity of *Oliver Twist* is the unity of London, in which the lives of riff-raff and of wealthy folk brush and sometimes entangle. In his portrayal of the city, Dickens passes no real judgement, as he does over the deeds of his characters. The London environment is never discussed in the stately, abstract way dear to many of his contemporaries. Rather, the highly individual idiosyncratic characters seem to bring their environment under their own power. They cannot change it, but they can make of it what they will as they make their ways through life.Dickens is no determinist; though he believes in private philanthropy to ease the conditions of the poor, he sees their lives as full of choices, just as more fortunate people's are.

The macabre

Sometimes the settings for criminal life become sensational in their brooding menace. Dreary poverty relieved by outbursts of violence seems to be a polluted atmosphere the characters are breathing. Some become victims, others aggressors. The evil done thickens the gloomy dark in which others will continue to live. By suggesting free will even in the midst of this, Dickens keeps the novel full of suspense – will Nancy assist Oliver, will Sikes murder Nancy, will Fagin escape death? – all these seem real questions, and as violent, sudden death closes in on all three, it seems to stalk them down. This excitement keeps a reader in a macabre state of horrified fascination into which Oliver's eventual rescue is like a sudden stream of light.

Perhaps the most terrible scene in the novel is Fagin's last encounter with Oliver. Brownlow's motives for bringing Oliver along to the prison puzzle a modern reader; does he trust the boy's natural goodness too much or too little? Possibly Dickens simply wanted the effect of such a dramatic clash between childhood innocence and mature, half-insane evil, thus ending the novel on a high emotional pitch. Perhaps he had an intuitive feeling for communicating the seriousness of Oliver's deprivations by such a sensational scene.

Domestic pastoral

In complete contrast to that tone is the mellow sweetness of Dickens's domestic scenes. They partake of the eighteenth-century pastoral's calm and good order. Lives of relatively unambitious simplicity are lived with a natural, unaffected grace that gives them beauty. The chief figures of this type are young women and eccentric, middle-aged bachelors. Happy marriage is anticipated for the women, but is only sketchily portrayed. In *Oliver Twist*, Rose Maylie lives such a life, protected by the goodness of Mrs Maylie and Dr Losberne. Her life has been bruised by the weak sin of her sister and the terrible malice of Monks and his mother, but her own personality has never been corrupted. Sickness and sacrifice are suffered by such characters, but they never seem to endure any difficult temptations. Yet Dickens does manage to suggest that their lives are economically and even physically protected by the harder work, and more difficult commitments of others. They are his only rather passive characters in novels crowded by good and evil of every description.

Characterisation

Oliver

A general rule about Dickens's characters is that they live gregariously–we know them best by the company they keep. Perhaps this is why Oliver's character seems something of a blank. The reader sees that he is too spirited to live among the defeated poor of the workhouse, and too virtuous to have anything but revulsion for a life of crime. He adapts happily and easily to the Brownlow household, and equally to the Maylies'. In each, he seeks a mother; Mrs Brownlow's old housekeeper and Rose both meet the small boy's need. We seldom see him with children of his own age; Dick is his only close friend. That part of his life, finding his own personality in the smaller world of a circle of friends, is denied him by the terrible circumstances of his life. Moreover, the special intimacy a small boy often has with his mother, or with the woman who mothers him, is replaced in Oliver's early life by institutions which show no real trace of human compassion. They do nothing to develop any personality in him. But perhaps in being still such a beginner at life, Oliver is Dickens's strongest argument against the workhouses as any substitute for individual care for the poor.

Mr Brownlow and Mr Grimwig

Like many of Dickens's adult characters, Mr Brownlow seems to be seen mainly through a child's vision. His eccentricities are all noticed, as if he were on the unreachable pedestal of secure respectability usually occupied by a child's teachers, or older relations. In fact, he becomes both teacher and adopted older relative to young Oliver, at the close of the novel. What he is like in himself we see only sketchily. Gradually we realise he has had passions of his own, and still feels deeply for the girl he lost, and the wayward friend who was Oliver's father. He is beyond middle age, but Oliver renews enough of youth in him to reawaken those moods of regret and tenderness that lay almost forgotten in his heart.

His counterpart, Mr Grimwig, is a fossilised character, someone caught in one state of mind and pictured as that always. He is kindly but testy, as a foil for Brownlow's more considered view of people.

In this respect Brownlow is a true gentleman, unwilling to hurt anyone who deserves protection, but severe, truly severe, when meeting real evil.

Nancy and Sikes

Nancy's half-starved emotions show the ravages of deprivation extended into adult life. She cannot remember a family life and cannot hope to create one. All her motherly instincts are battered by continually witnessing Fagin's horde of children trained for a hard, immoral life and perhaps an early death. Their camaraderie and hers are a brave show and an attempt to experience some warmth. But Nancy's needs are more mature; she also longs for a life-partner, a real marriage. She gives Sikes love, and never betrays his trust. She nurses him, protects him from

Fagin and from the law, and even throws away her own chance of a new life because she must not forsake him.

Dickens frequently defended portraying Nancy as sympathetically as he had, and perhaps within the novel itself, she is defended by the parallel to the more genteel fallen woman Agnes, who was Oliver's mother. They both suffer greatly in the unequal contest between men and women, and yet are not as guilty as the men they love. They both act out of misguided love, and both care for Oliver in a selfless way.

Sikes is a storm of violence rather than a character. We see few traits that could have caused Nancy's love. Nor is he capable of understanding her well enough to trust her against appearances. She haunts him after he kills her, but the violence of the crime itself may cause this. Dickens never suggests that Sikes realises Nancy did not betray him.

Rose Maylie and the Maylie household

Rose Maylie, the good, pure woman of the book, also suffers from the unequal way blame is distributed in society. She is actually of a decent family, but the deaths of her parents and fall of her sister have left her as a foundling who, malicious voices whisper, is illegitimate. Because of her sad beginning, she cannot accept the proposal of marriage Harry Maylie offers her without blighting his prospects. Yet woman as a lodestone of virtue is embodied by Dickens in Rose.

His love for Rose causes Harry Maylie to turn away from a bright political future, seeing its successes as shallow and all-dependent on foolish opinion. He takes up a better life, that of a quiet country clergyman, to gain her hand. Harry seems rather unrealistically drawn.

His mother, Mrs Maylie, is more convincing. She combines shrewdness and prudence with personal generosity. Without naïvely believing in the goodness of others, she does what she can to help all the young people become good.

Fagin

The red-haired Jew, whose filthy, scrawny appearance suggests miserliness, is at first almost a cartoon character. He rules over boys; he would never rule over men. He is like a caricature of an evil headmaster, whose boys are to graduate in crime, if they learn well enough to pass the test in the streets.

However, Dickens gradually hints and suggests that Fagin is more sinister than a reader might at first imagine. He does have considerable power over the women, especially those like Nancy whom he knew as children. He is capable of tormenting Bill Sikes, although Sikes could easily overpower him. His victims are demoralised and sometimes blackmailed, as he hopes to blackmail Nancy if he can persuade her to murder Sikes. The control he seeks is total, but dispassionate, for his victims mean nothing to him. Murder at a distance is easy enough for him to conscience.

Fagin's thoughts centre always on himself, a philosophy dazzling in its simplicity. This view of life is shared only by Noah Claypole, a repulsive character who lacks Fagin's cunning or capacity to take calculated risks.

Chapter 52, which describes Fagin's last days, opens his thoughts to the reader. In a brilliant way Dickens allows Fagin one last chance to appeal to the reader's pity. His fear of death is so paralysing that he seems only half-conscious, and it would be a hardened reader indeed who did not feel a shiver of sympathy for the trapped man. But Fagin does die, and although what capital crime he was charged with is not made clear, the reader may feel that natural justice has been served.

The Bumbles

Claiming virtue, despite dedicated self-seeking, is the prerogative of the Bumbles. The public face of public charity is never attractive in Dickens's novels, but the Bumbles are particularly obnoxious because they deal with children, and with the old. Each Bumble is shown to be a bully, though Mr Bumble is quick to turn coward when he meets his match. Mrs Bumble is another sort of bully, the kind who, in the last resort, looks for a scapegoat to blame. She is also more of a schemer than her unlucky husband, and can take the credit for the doubtful initiatives that land them in so much trouble. She takes the pawn-ticket from the dead workhouse inmate and redeems it without her husband's knowledge. She settles a price with Monks for destroying the evidence of Oliver's identity. She is attracted, not just to the appearance of power, but to its casual, cruel exercise.

In creating the Bumbles, Dickens was attacking the administration of the Poor Laws, which took its tone from the Reform legislation itself. The deserving poor were to be distinguished from the feckless and idle. Hardship and shame were to accompany any relief. In the 1830s relieving the poor was seen only as a religious obligation, not as a civic duty. Unemployed people were not seen as members of a society which had failed to give them means of livelihood. In some way they were outside society, preying upon it. The Bumbles and their kind were the barrier between respectable society and the needy, and therefore always made their sympathies and social standing clear. In a peculiar twist of revenge, the Bumbles lose all hope of work and end up in the very workhouse they once ran.

Monks

Monks is the silent figure of menace in the novel. Until Chapter 40, when Nancy relates to Rose what she overheard Monks say to Fagin, Dickens does not give away Monks's real identity as Oliver's half-brother. Only at the close of the novel, when Brownlow confronts Monks, does the reader fully penetrate his sinister motives. He wishes Oliver's soul as black as his own, for the sheer joy of it, as well as for the inheritance he will get if Oliver disgraces himself.

Monks's strange appearance with Fagin at Oliver's study window in Mrs Maylie's country cottage, suggests to the reader how deep an impression the evil men have made on the child's mind. They come, like dream figures, when he is asleep. He wakens in fright, and is convinced he sees them run away, but no footsteps are made in the soft ground, and their visit is not explained until the very end of the novel. It is like the other incident in which Oliver espies from Losberne's carriage the house in which he was kept by Fagin, but when Losberne investigates, the house has another occupant. Though Dickens does not imply that Oliver is mistaken, he leaves the reader to wonder if Oliver will always be haunted by sudden reminders of the evil which sought to destroy him.

Monks himself suffers, for he is twisted and crippled by the evil desires he longs to gratify. He gets fits, and cannot bear to be alone. He tells Bumble during a storm, 'Not all the rain that ever fell, or ever will fall, will put as much of hell's fire out, as a man can carry about with him' (Chapter 38). Given a last chance by Brownlow, he squanders everything again, in the years that follow the events of the novel. He is a lost soul.

Dickens's literary milieu

Dickens had a popular imagination crammed with the sorts of lore ordinary people shared. He admired the works of Sir Walter Scott, whose long historical novels were immensely popular. They are romantic, but never grotesquely humorous, as Dickens's novels often are. He had read the eighteenth-century novelists Fielding, Sterne, and Smollett, but a stronger impression in his young mind was made by the grandiosity of stage melodrama. Popular melodrama, always romantic and sensational, was usually blessed with a distinctly happy ending. Dickens knew the public was generally delighted when all turned out well for the long-suffering heroes and heroines, after all their trials had proved their worth. The plot of *Oliver Twist* owes more to these productions, and to the childhood fairytales in which brave young people endure the cruelty of evil adults, than it does to the episodic novels of the eighteenth century.

Dickens's sense of London comes from his own experience of the city's many sections. Perhaps a debt to the 'Newgate' novelists who glamorised crime and low life should be acknowledged, but Dickens's description is harsher and more saddening. Books such as Pierce Egan's (1772–1849) *Life in London* (1821) praised the rich diversity of the city without allowing the heroes to be hurt, or worse still corrupted, by any of it. Dickens portrayed individuals at risk in the city, and did not hesitate to show that some, like Nancy, could not escape its foulness.

Looking at all this life from a child's viewpoint is Dickens's own invention. It removes the books from politics but not from compassion. Social customs, including those which govern property, and sexual bonding, are seen with the all-accepting fatalism of childhood. Dickens does interject his own opinions in expostulations from time to time, but abstract thinking is avoided; everything is concrete, immediate, and emotionally urgent.

An influence Dickens himself pointed out in his 1841 preface to *Oliver Twist* was the work of William Hogarth (1697–1764). This great artist, Dickens said, was his only predecessor in treating of the miserable realities of poor criminal life. Hogarth was admired by many early nineteenth-century writers, but Dickens took this admiration a step further, in supervising illustrations for his own writing with minute care.

Dickens loved the theatre all his life, even though nineteenth-century English theatre was mainly poor in quality; undemanding melodrama and farce were its staples. Dickens longed to involve himself in theatre; he made theatrical friends, most notably the actor William Charles Macready (1793–1873), and he tried amateur dramatics. His books were sometimes pirated into plays (usually rather badly), but this did not dampen his personal love of the sensationalism of theatre, or of its immediacy, its intimate contact with an audience. In his later years, he gave public readings, touring both in England and America.

Earlier this need was satisfied by serialised writing. All but *Hard Times*, *A Tale of Two Cities*, and *Great Expectations* began life as monthly serials; they came out in weekly parts. Many of the famous nineteenth-century novelists wrote this way; readers wrote to them, offering suggestions, and weekly or monthly sales reflected the level of readers' enthusiasm. If sales fell, new characters could be brought in, or the plot enlivened by a tour of a foreign country, or a sudden crisis.

Dickens always accepted that as a novelist he was partly a popular entertainer. He had no artistic qualms about wanting to please his readers. But by sheer imaginative energy, he often overtook their ideas, and carried them to a perception of social problems, and to a wider experience of social life, than they could have had by themselves.

Perhaps he did this by appearing to write with the directness and innocence of a highly imaginative child, who cannot imagine why bad things are allowed to happen. He also allowed emotions to dominate scenes of suffering. Particular stories are allowed to tell themselves in all their force and peculiarity. This seeming restraint from judgement gave him a wide readership, left him as no group's partisan, in the intense and confused social struggles which industrialisation had brought to English life.

Finally, it must be said that Dickens's love of grotesque humour, which everyone remembers as his dominant mode, fuses so remarkably with the physicality of his characters that they are like the real-life trolls and gremlins of folk-lore, and have the same indisputable right to exist for ever. Although he portrayed his time, he did it in this way, and made near-fairytale, instead of politics.

Historical setting

During the nineteenth century England became rapidly industrialised. This led to vast social movement from the country villages to the industrial centres. The people who came from the villages to the cities often did not find work. Then they could only slip into the vast whirlpool of the unemployed. They lived in a network of dark, dirty streets of ramshackle buildings, a maze which the wealthy never penetrated. Here were the dark wellsprings of crime.

The prosperous Victorians had a great pride in their industrial achievements, which they demonstrated at the Great Exhibition of 1851, for which they built a Crystal Palace to display manufactured goods. But with that pride they had a growing unease that this wealth would founder on the muck-heap of the miseries of the poor, which supported it. Although few of them understood the extent to which the colonies' cheap raw materials were creating English wealth, many could not hide from themselves the knowledge that cheap labour was contributing to cheap manufacture.

Dickens, who knew this more clearly than most, came to hate London; though he loved the gentle way of life its better classes enjoyed, he wanted that life somehow to be fused with the rural order, which had not so oppressed the poor. In *Oliver Twist*, the goodness of Mr Brownlow is enhanced by his natural attraction to the simple life of the country, an attraction shared by the Maylie household and perpetuated by the new life Rose and Harry take up, at the novel's close. However, cities had a fascination for Dickens, in their humanly expressive landscape and the multitude of rather warped personalities who inhabited their nooks and crannies. Dickens's imagination tended to see people and their places as changing together, both expressing what life is being experienced there. Change the place, and the person may be changed. They grow together like a tortoise's soft body and its carapace.

The empty country may have soothed him, but it did not irritate his imagination into effort. Perhaps he needed partly to dislike and to caricature what he wrote about. His sympathetic descriptions often seem vacuous.

Many upper-class Victorians were convinced that they were in the sway of a great force, a daemon progress. To it they attributed a merciless exercise of power worthy of a Greek tragedian's notion of Fate. In many cultivated minds, progress was an idea amalgamating the compelling moral force of Old Testament Jehovah, guiding the people to a better way of life, and the terrible, irresistible grip of destiny about which the Greek and Roman writers sometimes wrote. These two literatures, the Hebraic and the Classical, were the basic education of Victorian gentlemen. Dickens was remarkably free of all this, possibly because of his own erratic education and rather random reading. He disliked theorists of any persuasion. The English faith in progress he caricatured for its cruelty. The very titles of two of his later novels, *Hard Times* and *Bleak House*, suggest how far removed he was from this false and easy optimism. The American version of such notions he ridiculed in *Martin Chuzzlewit*. Instead of all this, Dickens turned to individual compassion, and a steady social order in which luckier, higher classes tried to be responsive as a matter of idealism to the needs of the poor. But he also disliked the bureaucratic boards and organisations his times produced to alleviate common miseries; attacking the Poor Laws in *Oliver Twist* is only one example of his general mistrust.

Summary of Dickens's achievement in *Oliver Twist*

Oliver Twist is a remarkably well-loved book. Generations of readers have read it with pleasure and remembered it with affection long after they closed it. This is a great achievement for any writer, and one which Dickens would have been delighted to foresee. But the real achievement of the book's imaginative force is that its impression of English life is absorbed into the unconscious heritage of the past and remains fused with it for ever. Most readers cannot think of nineteenth-century London without the characters that Dickens created walking its noisy streets, watching from its dusty windows, or busily talking. Although the characters are not drawn with great complexity, they also satisfy a reader's need to categorise the people he scarcely knows in his own life. They are drawn with such energy and enjoyment, even when it is the gusto of hearty dislike that is energising the portrayal, that the multiplicity of characters becomes bearable, and even entertaining. Easily roused to humour or pathos, the writer moves from one scene to the next, and from one mood to the next, with amazing speed. The reader may feel a little dizzy, but he is unlikely to be bored. In this way, the feel of urban life is exactly caught. Its emotional tempo, crowded with incidents, observations, and sudden plateaux of waiting, is so perfectly captured by the book that a connection with the real past is made at the deep level in which the reader experiences his own life. Perhaps it would be true to say that a reader who had never walked through a city would find Dickens's writing less familiar than one who had at least visited a city would, but he would still recognise that it had the same strangeness, the same difference from his own life, that the city has. Dickens includes rural scenes. In their contrast to other chapters, they seem like a holiday from the real business of the novel.

Dickens humanised the middle-class English perception of the urban poor, by showing their variety, and their irrepressible vitality. But the far-reaching impact of his sympathy was muddled by his attack on the vices of the lower-middle class. Poor people whose lot improves usually become lower-middle-class, yet Dickens does not make that seem a desirable state in life. Their lives seem more narrow and exacting even when they are not also more pretentious, than those of the unlucky poor. In fact, Dickens never manages to make working for a living seem very attractive. Although he took a fierce pride in financially lifting his family out of the doldrums of the half-employed, Dickens retained a certain horror of the drudgery which constricts those who work, until their very personalities seem to grow into the moulds of their jobs, and their original features are slightly, grotesquely changed.

Dickens writes totally without guilt himself; he sees his material with a direct freshness that makes his work quite different from most social novelists. What he sees is put down in the heat of that moment's emotions and then the man and the mood move on, changing as they go. A deep basic sympathy for life underlies many of his perceptions and unifies them, but their variety is as striking an impression on the reader as is the unifying sympathy. Life and death are both accepted, even though life is cherished and death is feared. Dickens's choice of youngsters as heroes and heroines is a natural outgrowth of his style. It is also part of his achievement, for he, together with that other nineteenth-century giant William Wordsworth (1770–1850), created a new understanding of the intense, receptive quality of a child's soul. In *Oliver Twist*, the first of his young heroes takes on the task of making his own life, choosing among the ways of life he has seen, and deeply understood. For such an extroverted book, one concerned more with external than internal realities, *Oliver Twist* casts a long shadow; the shadow is the man that may be, running alongside the child who is.

Finally, *Oliver Twist* initiated the activity of plotting books as plays were plotted, with a moral urgency to their action. Even Jane Austen

(1775–1817) seems to be making a dispassionate observation of interesting social episodes, in comparison to Dickens, but later nineteenth-century novelists expect significance from the conflicts in their plots, significance manifest in an emotionally stirring way. They wish to teach the heart more than they want to sharpen the wits.

One cannot come to the end of a great creative genius. Different experiences in their own lives cause readers to appreciate different aspects of the author's achievement. Dickens's view of life has become part of the way many people see life. That is an influence so profound that its effects are still with us, happening weekly, whenever a social worker or a politician describes someone living 'in Dickensian conditions' or strikes a pose as the bluff, benevolent type of do-gooder whom Dickens seems to trust. In the British Isles Dickens is a living force, conditioning relations between the classes. Read by many people who read few other good novelists, referred to at least once in almost any Sunday newspaper, or magazine, Dickens is now part of the popular lore he respected. His imaginative habits have become part of the mental habits of the British people.

Part 4

Hints for study

(1) The themes of the novel will emerge from the lives of the characters, as the reader watches what happens. For this reason close attention to the complicated plot is a good beginning when the student tries to interpret the book. The book is social in its themes, so a precise grasp of each character's social role is necessary to understand the judgements Dickens makes about his or her moral behaviour. Different characters have different ranges of moral possibility; purity is impossible for Nancy and pride will never tempt Rose. Both may atrophy from despair; despair is their crisis, and their social link. Taking care to give the characters' social situations close attention, the reader soon realises that this book has many themes, no one of them dominant. It is no parable, but a portrait of many lives.

(2) Different readers may sense the climax of the book at different points. The scene in which Nancy betrays Monks to Rose Maylie and Mr Brownlow, thus rescuing Oliver and redeeming her own soul, represents the turn of the tide. But it is just that: a tide turning, and slowly becoming a stronger force against the beach. Moral energy, quickened by love, will now rescue the child and save Nancy's spirit from total destruction. Oliver, the hero of the book, is not even present in the scene. His childhood vulnerability and passivity are never more obvious than when the adults group to save him. If the novel is seen as primarily his story, this is a curious climax.

Another climax of excitement is the earlier scene in which Nancy gains entry to Rose's hotel room, and the two societies, poor and protected, meet on adult terms. This is foreshadowed by Oliver's earlier encounters with Mr Brownlow and the Maylies, but he has the potentialities of childhood to interest their sympathies. If the novel is seen primarily as a social study, this meeting is its climax. However, in no other sense is Rose a major character. She is no guardian of the social order, but part of what it protects. The harm society has done her makes her more open to Nancy's suffering than she would have been without any personal experience of humiliation. She stands as an ambivalent representative of her society, protected but harmed, and instinctively wiser in her generosity than it is, in its prejudiced consolidation.

(3) The setting, London, may be seen as giving the real unity to the book that its melodramatic plot and its unformed central character cannot quite give. In *Oliver Twist*, an unformed personality resonates between two great centres of energy, the criminal world, and the moneyed society who dictate the accepted social order. London contains both these energies, and many lives lived within their influence in its own teeming complex life. It represents possibilities, not just background.

(4) The unequal contests in the book do not represent anyone's inner conflict between good and evil, with the possible exception of Nancy's struggle. Oliver is called upon for stamina rather than decisiveness. The moral energy of the good is individual, and in turn, good characters are menaced by bad characters. However, throughout the story evil is aided by casual cruelty and indifference. A reader gradually sees the complex nature of social evils portrayed amusingly and with devastating accuracy.

(5) The characters are created out of their gestures and language. Few inner monologues occur in Dickens's pages. You may find some of the characters a little sketchy and cartoon-like. This verges on caricature, a term you could explore in connection with Dickens.

(6) The place of children in the book is unusual in English fiction. Unprotected and exploited children haunted Dickens's imagination. A reader needs to feel, as well as think, his way into Dickens's emotions and attitudes about this subject. The adult world to Dickens seemed like a sophisticated country through which a child might make his way as a foreigner would in a strange land. Frightened misunderstandings, false courage and bravado are his real enemies in his struggle to keep alive. Growing is random and half-stunted. The unloved children often seem a little withered; critics have called them Dickens's 'old children': too wise, in a limited way; and no longer growing in other ways. Perhaps one of Dickens's powerful attractions for adults is that almost all adults feel they were a little hurried into responsibilities. Dickens sees that, with deep sympathy, and stirs our pity for those unready for the only life open to them.

(7) A reader needs to be patient with Dickens's notion of good women. It is more the sketch of a human need for fulfilment than of any possible character. The older, shrewder, good women are more interesting characters than the young rosebud girls. Dickens was sensing in young men a need for chivalry and protectiveness that would stimulate their energy in doing their duties. Duty is an important concept to Dickens, but he understands it mainly from a male viewpoint. He does not understand how complex a woman's sense of duty can be.

Specimen questions and hints for answering them

When you are working on essays in an examination, or in a more leisured situation, remember the question is specific. Don't write down everything you know about Dickens; read the question several times. Think of a main idea which replies to that question, and develop it roughly in notes. Expand this idea, refine it, point out any possible objections to it, and reply to them, or go on to a related idea. However, you must see your answer as an essay, with its own points to make, and its own need for a fluent, clear style.

Here are a few sample questions and possible answers, in outline.

---

(1) *Oliver Twist* is a novel in which the main character is a child. Does this strengthen or weaken the book?

The question is about structure in a novel. Does a novel need a dominant main character? Can the themes of a novel develop clearly without such a character to bring them into focus? Can the plot, particularly in such a long novel, avoid confusion or inanity with the immature thoughts of a child as the main reflection of the action? You will want to form a definite opinion about some of these issues before you attempt an answer. Other possible points to consider include whether such an unusual vantage-point gives the book pathos and poignancy, and whether it makes the caricatures seem more innocent, or more biting. You will certainly think of other points related to the peculiar strengths of Dickens's style. With such an entertaining and skilful writer your difficulties may come more in organising your thoughts than in thinking of things to say.

---

(2) Is the historical background in *Oliver Twist* convincing? Is it meant to be?

This question enters the difficult area of the author's intentions and requires some sophisticated handling. It distinguishes between journalism (the reportage of fact) and fiction (the creation of stories related to fact only in ways that the author deems appropriate). There would be different connections between the real world and the fictional world in the works of different authors. Did Dickens, like some other nineteenth-century novelists, see himself as having a duty to report bad social conditions? Did his newspaper background influence his writing? Or was he predominantly involved in creating a world where moral truths could be more obvious than they are in ours, and where goodness and beauty are linked? These are deep questions. You will need to think hard before you write. Points to consider will include the significance of the setting in Dickens's creation of the atmosphere of the story, and the realism or improbability of the eventual outcome of the story.

---

(3) In what way does Dickens break new ground for the novel in *Oliver Twist*?

To answer this question you need a fairly thorough knowledge of novels written before *Oliver Twist* and some grasp of the book's influence on later writers. Dickens manages to use different moods within one novel; the grim, satirical opening, the lively good humour of scenes involving Mr Grimwig or Dr Losberne, the pathetic, touching scenes of Oliver's distress, and the sweet romantic moments Rose and Harry share give the novel a new range and require a new basis for internal unity. You may wish to consider how *Oliver Twist* derives its unity. Alternatively, you may look at particular writers before Dickens, and contrast his work to theirs, in its plot structure, its range of characters, or its themes and moral tone.

---

(4) Dickens is often at his most funny when he is at his most biting. Comment, using examples from *Oliver Twist*.

This question is a relatively easy one, as it deals directly with the text of the novel. You could take a few examples: Mr Bumble conversing with the woman who rears the parish young; Mr Bumble wooing Mrs Corney; Oliver daring to ask for more food at the workhouse. However, you could also be more ambitious, and then discuss the dual nature of comedy, its other aspect of sadness, or of anger, that gives it a serious purpose beyond entertainment. You could ask how the comic moments of *Oliver Twist* relate to other moments in the novel, when other moods prevail.

---

(5) Dickens's minor characters are sketchy cartoons. Are the major ones differently drawn?

This is a fascinating question if you are really interested in novels, because it relates to the techniques of one of England's great novelists which most distinguish his works from other great novels. Dickens created in prose a type of character sketching that had parallels only in earlier woodcut drawings or sketches, not in fiction. The slightly grotesque characters who demonstrate a way of life in a gesture, or a lifelong attitude or lifelong hypocrisy in a repeated phrase, are Dickens's particular mode of dealing with the plethora of people one cannot know well. But his central characters are not richly drawn, though they are treated with more sentiment and more seriousness. For this reason they never dominate the book, as a central character created by, say, George Eliot (1819–80), or W. M. Thackeray (1811–63) does. We seldom hear them speak original thoughts. If we did, perhaps the terrific sense of life's abundance, and the playful feeling of adventure that give Dickens's novels zest, would be lessened. We would leave the streets, and enter the private thoughts and feelings of other people.

Yet the fact that they are accorded some measure of respectful seriousness enables Dickens to use their sorrows as suggestions of social themes. He also allows the young people who make their way in a wicked world to show both the dangers besetting all innocence, and the courage and persistence needed to acquire serenity, and to begin their real achievements.

Part 5

Suggestions for further reading

The text

A full edition of Dickens's works currently in print is the *Oxford Illustrated Dickens*, published by Oxford University Press, Oxford. The most recent edition of *Oliver Twist* was published in 1978. A good paperback edition is published by Penguin Books, Harmondsworth, 1966 (many reprints); the student using the latter edition will notice the slightly different arrangement of Chapters 12 and 13.

Critical works

CHESTERTON, G. K.: *Charles Dickens*, Methuen, London, 1906. A famous early critical study by a lively essayist and fellow novelist.

COLLINS, PHILIP: *Dickens and Crime*, Macmillan, London, 1965. This sorts out the fact and the fiction in Dickens's treatment of Victorian crime and punishment.

FORSTER, JOHN: *The Life of Charles Dickens*, Chapman and Hall, London, 1872–4. The authorised life by Dickens's oldest friend.

GREAVES, JOHN: *Dickens at Doughty Street*, Hamish Hamilton, London, 1975. This recounts Dickens's life while living at 48 Doughty Street, 1837–9, the period in which *Pickwick Papers* and *Oliver Twist* were finished, *Nicholas Nickleby* was written, and *Barnaby Rudge* begun. It is good on details of his publication contracts.

HOUSE, HUMPHREY: *The Dickens World*, Oxford University Press, London, 1941. An early historical study of Dickens in his period.

JOHNSON, E.: *Charles Dickens: His Tragedy and Triumph*, revised and abridged, Allen Lane, London, 1977. This is probably the definitive biography.

MILLER, J. HILLIS: *Charles Dickens: the World of His Novels*, Indiana University Press, Bloomington, 1969. An attempt to portray Dickens's interior 'imaginative universe', through scrutiny of his style and recurrent images.

WILSON, ANGUS: *The World of Charles Dickens*, Penguin Books, Harmondsworth, 1972. A full and lively account of Dickens's career, with interesting critical remarks, by a fellow novelist.

The author of these notes

SUZANNE BROWN completed a BA in English 'with honour and distinction' at Mount Holyoke College in Massachusetts. She has a diploma in Anglo-Irish literature from Trinity College, Dublin, where she received her PH D in 1975. She also has a higher diploma in education. She has worked as a part-time lecturer and tutor in Trinity College. She is the author of Hawthorne's *The Scarlet Letter* in the York Notes series. She has also published poetry and essays on educational matters.

York Notes: list of titles

HENRY FIELDING
Joseph Andrews
Tom Jones

F. SCOTT FITZGERALD
Tender is the Night
The Great Gatsby

E. M. FORSTER
A Passage to India
Howards End

ATHOL FUGARD
Selected Plays

JOHN GALSWORTHY
Strife

MRS GASKELL
North and South

WILLIAM GOLDING
Lord of the Flies
The Inheritors
The Spire

OLIVER GOLDSMITH
She Stoops to Conquer
The Vicar of Wakefield

ROBERT GRAVES
Goodbye to All That

GRAHAM GREENE
Brighton Rock
The Heart of the Matter
The Power and the Glory

THOMAS HARDY
Far from the Madding Crowd
Jude the Obscure
Selected Poems
Tess of the D'Urbervilles
The Mayor of Casterbridge
The Return of the Native
The Trumpet Major
The Woodlanders
Under the Greenwood Tree

L. P. HARTLEY
The Go-Between
The Shrimp and the Anemone

NATHANIEL HAWTHORNE
The Scarlet Letter

SEAMUS HEANEY
Selected Poems

ERNEST HEMINGWAY
A Farewell to Arms
For Whom the Bell Tolls
The African Stories
The Old Man and the Sea

GEORGE HERBERT
Selected Poems

HERMANN HESSE
Steppenwolf

BARRY HINES
Kes

HOMER
The Iliad

ANTHONY HOPE
The Prisoner of Zenda

GERARD MANLEY HOPKINS
Selected Poems

WILLIAM DEAN HOWELLS
The Rise of Silas Lapham

RICHARD HUGHES
A High Wind in Jamaica

THOMAS HUGHES
Tom Brown's Schooldays

ALDOUS HUXLEY
Brave New World

HENRIK IBSEN
A Doll's House
Ghosts
Hedda Gabler

HENRY JAMES
Daisy Miller
The Europeans
The Portrait of a Lady
The Turn of the Screw
Washington Square

SAMUEL JOHNSON
Rasselas

BEN JONSON
The Alchemist
Volpone

JAMES JOYCE
A Portrait of the Artist as a Young Man
Dubliners

JOHN KEATS
Selected Poems

RUDYARD KIPLING
Kim

D. H. LAWRENCE
Sons and Lovers
The Rainbow
Women in Love

CAMARA LAYE
L'Enfant Noir

HARPER LEE
To Kill a Mocking-Bird

LAURIE LEE
Cider with Rosie

THOMAS MANN
Tonio Kröger

CHRISTOPHER MARLOWE
Doctor Faustus
Edward II

ANDREW MARVELL
Selected Poems

W. SOMERSET MAUGHAM
Of Human Bondage
Selected Short Stories

J. MEADE FALKNER
Moonfleet

HERMAN MELVILLE
Billy Budd
Moby Dick

THOMAS MIDDLETON
Women Beware Women

THOMAS MIDDLETON and WILLIAM ROWLEY
The Changeling

ARTHUR MILLER
Death of a Salesman
The Crucible

JOHN MILTON
Paradise Lost I & II
Paradise Lost IV & IX
Selected Poems

V. S. NAIPAUL
A House for Mr Biswas

SEAN O'CASEY
Juno and the Paycock
The Shadow of a Gunman

GABRIEL OKARA
The Voice

EUGENE O'NEILL
Mourning Becomes Electra

GEORGE ORWELL
Animal Farm
Nineteen Eighty-four